Praise
Jeremy Robert Johnson
&
All the Wrong Ideas

"A master of mood, seamlessly combining the literary with the grotesque. Johnson deserves to be a household name..."

—**Publishers Weekly**

"Genre-bending...haunting..."

—**The Washington Post**

"Johnson captures humanity's absurdity, our grotesqueries, sometimes our triumphs, all the while pushing past the limits of reality, transforming it into something dark, and surreal, and unforgettable."

—**B&N Sci-Fi & Fantasy Blog**

"[A] fantastic new voice in mainstream fiction..."

—**Los Angeles Review of Books**

"A powerful imagination, a great talent for storytelling, writing chops that allow him to tackle any genre, and a flowing, dynamic voice that, if Johnson were a singer, would extend to an impressive eight octaves."

—**Electric Literature**

"Surreal, visceral, and frequently unsettling...One more descriptor, while we're at it: highly entertaining. Johnson brings a pulpy urgency to the page, which blends neatly with the frequently heady concepts that he utilizes in his fiction."

—**Tor.com**

"Johnson writes with an energy that propels you through some very dark spaces indeed and into something profoundly unsettling but nonetheless human."

—**Brian Evenson**, author of *A Collapse of Horses*

"Reading Johnson, you feel you are in the grip of an immensely powerful, possibly malevolent, but fiercely intelligent mind."

—**Nick Cutter**, author of *The Troop*

"I've seen the future and it's bizarre, it's beautifully berserk, it's Jeremy Robert Johnson."

—**Stephen Graham Jones**, author of *The Only Good Indians*

"Jeremy writes like his brain is on fire and he's in no rush to put it out."

—**Paul Tremblay**, author of *Survivor Song*

"A dazzling writer."

—**Chuck Palahniuk**, author of *Fight Club*

"One of the most exciting voices in contemporary fiction. Jeremy Robert Johnson's work has always tested the limits of both genre and literary fiction."

—**Bookslut**

"Jeremy Robert Johnson is dancing to a way different drummer. He loves language, he loves the edge, and he loves us people. *This* is entertainment...and literature."

—**Jack Ketchum**, author of *The Girl Next Door*

"Waaaay out at the deep end of the collective unconscious—where even the bravest of brain cells fear to tread—Jeremy Robert Johnson performs stand-up comedy for the gods. And their laughter is a marvelous, terrible thing. He's the kind of post-Lovecraftian genius berserker who makes the Great Old Ones new again. As with Clive Barker, there is no glorious mutational eruption that Johnson can't nail directly through your gawping mind's eye."

—**John Skipp**, NY Times Bestselling author of *Spore* (w/Cody Goodfellow) and *The Bridge* (w/Craig Spector)

"Not unlike David Foster Wallace's wicked and perhaps deranged younger brother."

—**21C Magazine**

"The guy's a genius. Reminds me of William Gibson—the dark interest in altered states of consciousness, the unrelentingly furious forward movement, and the same kind of unlimited imagination."

—**Ben Loory**, author of *Stories for Nighttime* and *Some for the Day*

"Johnson weaves vivid and fascinatingly grotesque tales."

—**Bookgasm**

"In its most twisted moments, Johnson's writing is too gleeful to pigeon-hole as strictly horror, and when he steps outside the gross-out game he transcends most other straight literary writers."

—Verbicide

"I don't know if Mr. Johnson sold his soul to the devil to give him this gift for nightmare imagery, but by god, this guy can write. Johnson excels at pathology and perversity. A confirmed weirdo and authentic writer of uncommon emotional depth who deserves to be watched."

—Cemetery Dance

All the Wrong Ideas

Jeremy Robert Johnson

Coevolution Press
Portland, OR

Coevolution Press
Portland, OR

WWW.JEREMYROBERTJOHNSON.COM
ISBN: 978-1-7367815-2-4

"Amniotic Shock in the Last Sacred Place" originally appeared in Pain and Other Petty Plots to Keep You in Stitches. "Ex-Hale," "Precedents," "Priapism," "Two Cages, One Moon," "Branded," and "Last Thoughts Drifting Down" originally appeared in Angel Dust Apocalypse. "Sparklers Burning" originally appeared at HORRORFIND: Fiction. "Wall of Sound: A Movement in Three Parts" originally appeared as "Liquidation" in Happy #15, "Deeper" in Glass Tesseract Vol. #3, and "A Number of Things Come to Mind" in Happy #17. "Extinction Journals" was originally published as a standalone novella via Swallowdown Press. "Working at Home" originally appeared in THE EDGE: Tales of Suspense #18. "The Witness at Dawn," "The Brilliant Idea," "Cortical Reorganization," and "The Encore" originally appeared in Cemetery Dance #60. "Consumerism" originally appeared in Falling From the Sky. "Trigger Variation" originally appeared in The Vault of Punk Horror. "Simple Equations" originally appeared in A Dark and Deadly Valley. "Laws of Virulence" originally appeared in Warmed and Bound. "The Seat of Reason" originally appeared in Fangoria Vol 2, Issue #6. Longstanding thanks to all editors and publishers involved in the original publication of these stories.

Book design and typeset ©2021 by Matthew Revert.
Printed in the USA.

Contents

For You
(Though *possibly* not You, not at this moment in time. No guarantees. Each book requires such a miraculous confluence of experience, thought, and perception between two human minds that it's dizzying to imagine how any fictive work might actualize inside another brain as something resonant and desired and wildly rewarding. But some books have been for Me, so there's a chance that this one, maybe, just maybe, is for You.)

Diametric Opposition:

An Introduction by Jeremy Robert Johnson

If you told me it was bad for me then I couldn't have wanted it more. Nihilistic gangster rap with that mentally magnetic Explicit Warning sticker, books which had been banned or hidden on my parents' highest shelves, movies that were rumored to have prompted real-life homicide investigations...I had to have it all. Unrated? Uncensored? A grainy VHS dub of the rare German Laserdisc of some movie too "dangerous" to be distributed in the States?

Hook it to my veins.

Those were the dark woods of my childhood. That was *adventure*...mowing the lawn with Ice Cube's Death Certificate on my Walkman, hiding Naked Lunch and Soul on Ice at the bottom of a cardboard box in my closet. That was me, taking temporary bug-out escapes from my world as a frail book nerd in a too-small town, dodging the bargain-bin brutality of daily life by indulging in whatever fully, transcendently transgressive thing I could get my grubby little hands on.

It was great, except for all the times it wasn't. Because that's the thing with adventures...there's quicksand out there. Things that bite. You don't always come back the same. The end of *Exquisite Corpse*, those real animals in the Italian cannibal movies, the Habitrail in *American Psycho*, Objectivism, pretty much everything I (slowly) downloaded from rotten.com—it's all still in there, fused to my cortex.

It's a mess.

But I wouldn't be the same without those adventures. I wouldn't have found my personal boundaries, or thought as much about the nature of morality, or had the opportunity to understand experiences outside the culturally bereft and homogenized cloister of my youth.

That's why I get concerned sometimes, when I see folks rushing and tumbling over each other to declare something simply problematic, to strip away the nuance and antagonism and exploration from art, and place its contents in diametric opposition as either purely good or purely bad (with themselves, of course, landing in publicly fashionable alignment with the former).

Don't worry. I'm not going to yell at this cloud for too long. Why waste your time? If you picked up this book in the first place then you probably aren't engaged with your literature in that puritanical, morally simplistic kind of way. You can tell the difference between depiction and endorsement. You know how to separate the author and their fictional characters. You can extrapolate themes and meaning and roll with ambiguity. You've travelled to some weird, wild spaces in books. You're ready for the next adventure, and somehow, today, that's led you to this book.

This fucking thing.

What even *is* this?

Definitely the strangest round up of my short stuff, ever. All the stories my New York editors want to keep underground for a variety of sound reasons. Some formative fiction written by a very troubled mostly nineteen-to-twenty-five-year-old guy who was trying to get all his trauma and obsessions down on paper (like that would control them).

These aren't the outright extremities of Lee, or Cooper, or Stokoe, but they're still plenty problematic and power-packed with triggers: self-harm, all forms of abuse and assault, grief, miscarriage, addiction. Lots of dead kids. Some casual late 90's nu-metal misogyny. And those are just the *ingredients*, to say nothing of how this thing is built: bizarre experiments, pastiches, tonal exercises, a novella written under deep sleep deprivation, questionable comedy, and, I swear, a spoken-word piece from the POV of a nuclear bomb.

It's wild. And sometimes a mess. But it's alive, I think. Reading back through it felt like listening to an early 4-track recording I made in my basement. It's raw, but oddly *earnest* too. I mean, writing the story "Liquidation" was the exorcism which pulled me out of a months-long period of suicidal ideation, and earned me my first paid publication. So for all the hunger and anger and ridiculousness…this is the weird shit that saved me. And though there are things here that make me want to go back in time and slap the hell out of twentysomething me, they are still intractably a part of who I am today. You only walk one path. These stories are part of mine.

All of which is to say, these are the escape routes I cooked up for myself when the woods I'd ventured into in real life got a little too dark. They're often fucked-up and definitely weird, but they mean a lot to me. And they're yours now. You took the risk. Bought the book. Borrowed it from a friend. Stole it from an enemy. Regardless of how you got here, it's your adventure now.

Godspeed. Good luck in there.

Amniotic Shock in the Last Sacred Place

The drugs were wearing off. James Toddle's mind slowly broke the surface of the soft purple ocean which had engulfed it. Consciousness crept back into his skull and threw its weight around, asserting its ugly but undeniable presence.

He felt straps pinning him to a cold metal table. He felt the persistent travel of insects across his skin. He felt reality setting in.

Reality was the last thing he wanted. Reality told him he was a grown man wearing a giant diaper. Reality told him he had a nasty habit of hurting the women from whom he so desperately desired love. Reality was adult judgments and adult institutions and adult terms like "pathological need" and "infantilism." Reality was a place where his need and his hunger were becoming harder and harder to satiate.

James became so mired in self-pity he didn't even notice the pervasive slaughterhouse smell of the air around him. The sickness of his surroundings meant little next to his loneliness and ever-present need for love and attention.

He was weeping crocodile tears onto pudgy pink cheeks when the dope tube descended from the ceiling. The metal nozzle slid between his lips and pumped his mouth full of chemicals and protein pulp. Instinctively, he began to nurse.

Soon he was sleeping like a newborn baby, calm as a lamb despite the shrieks and wet screams and locust swarms of laughter that echoed throughout the Facility. His lips were wrapped leech-tight around the rusted metal nozzle that fed him and filled his body with pain-killer and his mind with fever dreams.

The dream was almost always the same and had been since he could remember. He was small again and he was being held tight and kept warm because he was special. A cuter, more wondrous child had never been born. He was feeding and he could close his eyes and feel his mother's love flowing over him, and into him, through her soft milk.

Eventually, though, the feeding stopped, and he was still hungry. *So hungry*. He wanted more milk, more love, more attention. He bit down harder on the breast in his mouth. He clamped down until he felt flesh separate and a chunk of his mother was in his belly and then he felt something flowing, something hot and salty, and he swallowed deep and hoped it would never end.

It was the crinkling of the plastic diaper which gave her hope. Nurse Sebac turned toward the sound that echoed in the oily ear puddles on each side of her head. Her optic nerves, long since exposed by an accidental Procedure Frenzy, wiggled in the air before her face, and pulled in her sight like an extended snake's tongue would pull in smell.

A vision of loveliness lay there before her, held to the floating storage table by thin straps of what appeared to be rhino hide. She twitched nervously for a second, looking around the room, wondering if it was possible to be attacked by a skinned rhino twice in one week. "Bad odds," she whispered to herself, trying to remain calm enough to study the patient.

There on the table, wearing only an oversized plastic diaper, and smelling heavily of talcum powder, was one of the shiniest, softest men she'd ever seen. A cracked and leaking tube hung down from the ceiling and ended in the patient's mouth. He was suckling at it, his lips pulling a combination of benzerol and somnambuline into his throat.

Nurse Sebac stamped the bony heel of her foot into the fleshy, ovular Pad that glowed yellow in front of the patient's storage table. The Pad squeaked, glowed brighter yellow, and slimed away, leaving a shiny trail on the shattered Formica flooring beneath it. It slithered back a minute later with a clipboard stuck to its top. She lifted the clipboard from the Pad and then kicked the glowing yellow globule across the room, where it sunk into the wall, whinnying as it dissipated.

She read the patient profile, which was written backwards and contained the words "parquet," "luggage," and "immolation." The one important piece of information was located on the back of the profile sheet, spelled out with pink crayon. Below the heading marked "Your Name:" it read "James Toddle."

She would need to know his name when he woke in her hidden apartment, high in the upper floors of the Facility. She would need to know what to call the man in the giant diaper before the procedure could begin.

Nurse Sebac dragged James Toddle behind her, being sure to let his table bump into the shifting walls around her. She had removed his tubes and hoped that the lack of anesthetic and constant jostling would wake him by the time they reached her secluded Facility hideaway in the swaying upper reaches. She passed Crew members and staff during her ascension. Any questions about her movement of the patient were covered with a prefabricated lie.

"Backscatter has requested that I saturate this man with various waste products and then oil him up and set him out on Veranda 8."

At that point everyone who stopped her would ask the same question, to which she would respond, "Yes, that's where we're keeping the razor-beaked turtles these days."

It seemed reasonable.

She continued up flight after flight of sticky stairs, and thought about her new project. Nurse Sebac had to have her hobbies, like any other victim of the nine to five to three to nine workdays. "Hobbies keep you sane," she told herself.

"So I take a few patients here and there, what's the harm? It's not like a big Facility like this is going to miss a few piddling, worthless patients, what with the thousands they process every day. *Especially* after they cut my morphine back to the daily bucket, it's like they owe *me*. I'm doing them a favor and keeping this place running more efficiently. They should thank me for working my fingers to the bone. In fact, this is my third set of hands this year!"

Filled with self-righteousness (and enough norepinephrine to seriously jack a small island civilization) she rushed up the remaining five flights of stairs. She inhaled deep as she passed through clouds of methane and mosquitoes, knowing she was close to her front door. As she approached the door she felt a series of sick, wracking spasms tear through her body with the heat of phosphor. She retched onto her feet and felt the fluid slide between her toes. Thick with protein and jellyfish nematocysts, the vomit stung her skin before the floor absorbed it.

"This is ridiculous!" she thought. "If they reduce my morphine ration one more time…" The thought was cut short by another string of dopesick gut explosions, all white fire and needles.

Eventually she composed herself and continued dragging the man in the diaper.

Once she and the patient were finally inside she closed the door of her secret apartment behind her. The slamming of the door woke James Toddle. His waking was brief. The moment he saw Nurse Sebac looking back at him with the waving stalks of her optic nerves he returned to his blessed unconsciousness.

The seeping purple lights that crawled across Nurse Sebac's ceiling were infested with wasps, the result of a failed "Nest-to-Chest" hive transplant she'd tried to perform weeks before. She'd even coated the patient's lungs with wasp pheromones, but once she set the hive free they instantly swarmed her overhead lighting and defiled it. Now her lighting had a strange buzz to it, worse than the old fluorescents in some of the surgical theaters. The constant, taunting sound of the buzz, amplified by her pain-killer withdrawals, crept into her head and haunted her.

Buzzbuzz you'll never be a Doctor *buzzbuzz* you've failed again *buzzbuzz* nice legs, tadpole *buzzbuzz* who are you fooling *buzzbuzz* dilantin is for Doctors *buzzbuzz* ha, only twelve surgeries in and you couldn't keep him alive *buzzbuzz* we're reducing your dosage levels *buzzbuzz* you'll just have to make do with less.

"Less" was eating her alive! She needed the *steady*, gratuitous supply of chemicals enjoyed by the Surgeons. And why not? She was just as creative as they were. She was the one that came up with Arterial Spray-painting. She was the one who fed hunger stimulants to patient's tapeworms. Pearls before surgical swine.

She had toyed with the idea that appearing Surgeon-like might earn her some kind of sedative stipend. She had amputated her legs and rigged up an elaborate pulley system, trying to feign leglessness in the surgical theater. They spotted the ruse instantly and spent the afternoon playing tetherball with her suspended torso. When they were done playing with her they even reattached her damn legs, which was *so* embarrassing.

No, the only way to get any real attention around here was through the rendering of the patients. She'd have to create a true abomination, something so abhorrent that everyone would expect nature to destroy it at any moment.

She had a chance to show her superiors what she was capable of. That chance was resting on the floor with his thumb in his mouth, dreaming of something and nursing furiously hard. He was her grand and horrible infant, the perfect patient for her plan.

"Well," she thought "I better get to gettin' on with it."

She ground her jaw in determination, spit out a shattered tooth, and swung her leg forward as fast as she could into the soft midsection of James Toddle, patient-at-large.

"Borf!" he exclaimed, followed by, "Ooooooohhhhhh!"

Then he began to cry, all red-faced wailing and high decibel screeching.

He didn't stop crying until she force-fed him a tube of high-powered verdalax, known for its ability to trigger violent, gushing outbursts of truth (after, of course, the horrible onset of gut cramping).

She waited a few minutes for the medicine to invade. Then she asked one question and watched the floodgates open.

"James, how did you get here?"

Glassy-eyed and hypnotized, James Toddle let it all out in a great cathartic babble, a torrent of nonsense that left impact ripples in Nurse Sebac's ear puddles.

"I just, well, I like wearing diapers, and one of my Momma's, one of them that I paid for, back when I was a popular baby, she paid for the electrolysis so I could be officially baby-like, and you can get awful poor buying these oversized diapers, and I just like to nurse and they wouldn't let me wear my bonnet to work so I was all done for and the rubber pants were what I wanted and my little brother was born and they took away *my* diapers and gave them to *him*, and paid attention to *him*, and they didn't care about *me* anymore, 'cause I wasn't in the diapers, so then I paid *real close* attention to my little brother until his head was black and then I ran away and I was all alone again and then I met one of my new Mommas and she took me in and I fell in love with her and one night she wouldn't feed me so *I had to* eat some of her soft parts and then I got sent to a special hospital and they said I had an Edible Oedipal complex that was *really* complex, but at least at the hospital they let me wear my diapers as long as I kept making dirties in them, and then one day I woke up and the hospital wall was missing like it blew up, and the bricks were smoking, and a man with a metal cage over his mouth asked me if I wanted to go to a better hospital and then he stuck a pokey in me and I woke up here and now I'm with you and I hope you're my new Momster, 'cause I'm hungry, so hungry..."

James Toddle was drooling.

Nurse Sebac opened her arms and freed one sagging gray breast from her filthy scrubs. She leaned over James and put it in his mouth and squeezed it with her hand until thick black oil smelling of curdled milk sprayed into his throat. James lapped it up for his new Momster, basking in the udder attention until his throat grew numb and his brain was carpeted, and gravity lost its hold on everything.

The procedure went perfectly. Between periodic feedings of Nurse Sebac's obsidian dark and highly anesthetic milk, James Toddle was shrinking. She was giving him super-doses of atropherone, a regressive growth hormone originally used to shrink cows to "Kickin' Size." After six successful super-dosings, James was just the right size to fit in her new machine. Smaller than a bread basket, bigger than the average human brain.

Even with an ocean of anesthetic in his system, James Toddle looked uncomfortable shrinking to his desired baby size. He began to scream when the plates in his skull de-fused and separated, but a mottled gray teat ended his tantrum.

Nurse Sebac made sure he was awake when she pulled back the tarps in the corner of her room to reveal the machine she had built but never had a chance to test.

James Toddle's eyes flashed wide in their milky haze as he saw the unveiling.

"I call it The Woom, James. You, my lovely child, are the first to take it for a test drive."

It floated three feet above the floor, a grotesque amalgam of human skin, horse hide, solidified secretions, mortar, brick, viscera, and plastic tubing.

The Woom began to quiver as Nurse Sebac brought James Toddle closer.

She pinched his right cheek and said, "See you in nine minutes."

Nurse Sebac lifted a fleshy fold at the base of the machine and pushed James into The Woom.

A mucus plug coagulated into place beneath James Toddle and he felt the walls around him grow closer. Fluid rushed in and he found he could breathe the green and black ichors into his lungs. The fluid was filled with luminescent brine which labored away at creating the new James. He floated there, tiny, in the machine that was numbing him and reshaping him, and thought, "Finally, back where I belong."

Nine minutes later, he was re-born. A fissure opened in the base of the machine and belched him out with a few gallons of amniotic fluid. His eyes were fused together and his nose emerged from his forehead like an inverted sink spigot. His mouth was fish-thin, and he could barely breathe.

Nurse Sebac took one look at him and said, "Now, that simply won't do. You won't survive long enough for me to show the boys downstairs. I better run you through the seed cleaner."

She opened a metal door at the top of The Woom and placed him inside again. Ropes of intestine slid around him, squeezing out his breath. Cone spiders scuttled around him and sucked away his vital fluids. The brick walls on each side of him throbbed with the heat of a blast furnace and dried him until he was just a husk. He felt one of the spiders bore into the side of his head and pull *him* out of his skull, and he felt his consciousness being carried along and dropped down a long tube, back into the warmth and darkness at the base of The Woom. His consciousness, the germ of him, planted its seed and he grew. As he gestated he pictured himself as the perfect man, with a newscaster's hair and a car dealer's smile, someone so normal that all Moms would have to love him, and care for him forever. He tried to grow *just right*. Nine minutes later he was back in his new Momster's arms.

"Oh, James! The four external livers are fine, but that adorable blonde hair has got to go! Try harder this time. I've got to show those uppity floating fucks something spectacular or I'll never be able to advance!"

James felt Nurse Sebac's hands shaking as she picked him up.

No matter how many times James Toddle was born, he wouldn't come out just right. Sure, he'd have a vestigal wing here, a monstrous case of hydropedalism there, but parts of him remained cherubic in contrast. It was never enough for Nurse Sebac, who credited herself as a perfectionist. The remaining will of James Toddle, the part of him that really wanted a Mom to love him, counteracted the designs of The Woom just enough to subvert its intentions. He wanted a Momster, Nurse Sebac wanted a monster.

He was born with a scaly foot sticking out of his abdomen and a button nose. He was born with rosy cheeks and assholes for eyes.

James felt hungrier and more alone with each birth. When he had limbs he would reach for his new Mom and try to cling to her. On the forty-eighth birth he managed to wind a white and jellied tentacle around her waist, but she clipped it off with a rib saw and forced him back into the seed cleaner. On the ninety-fourth birth he burrowed halfway into her thigh with his new circular mouth, but she poured salt on him and he shriveled.

After the hundredth birth James gave up hope and was sick of being born again.

He had no options. No matter how he felt, he was still born.

Hope left him. Despair filled The Woom and his incarnations became more and more horrible. His one hundred and forty-fifth birth went perfectly.

At last! He saw her eyes flash with adoration and a mother's love.

"Oh my! Toothy phalluses, inverted eyes, an antler-shaped skull, and cleft palate! I'm the luckiest mother in the world! I can't wait to show you off!"

He could see her infected injection points were salivating, anticipating oxycontin appetizers.

He watched her recognize the mirrored hunger and need in his new, jet-black eyes.

She picked him up to feed.

James Toddle fed for two days, then abandoned her corpse. After he ate her heart he was positive that she had no more love to give. He had swallowed the source.

He blamed the cold Mother-husk on the floor for his newfound loneliness. If she really loved him she'd keep on giving. All he needed was to be fed, and loved, and cherished.

His new Mom had grown cold to him after time, like the others before her. This Mom had grown cold *and* stiff, so once again he was on his own. He would need to find another Mother, one who would recognize him for the tiny miracle he was and never stop the flow of food and love that he required. He'd just have to try harder. He'd have to be the perfect child.

He shambled along the halls of the Facility in search of a new Mom. He tried, in spite of the prolapsed colon hanging wet from his neck and the stinking fluid ejaculated from the pulsing flesh protruding from his mouth, to feel wondrous and sweet and treasured.

Love, after all, was his birthright.

Ex-Hale

I see a lot of familiar faces out there in the audience tonight. Friends, family, co-workers, loved ones. I'm sure that Ray would be glad you all showed up. Ray really appreciated all of you. Well, except for Mark Clemont.

Mark, what are you doing here? Get out! We're all waiting, Mark. Mark, just show some decency and go. Mark, Jesus Christ, no you can't see the body. No, you know it's closed casket only. Mark, do us all a favor and go before we have to call security. Are you drunk, Mark? Look, man, now Ray's mom is crying. Yeah, well I guess we can't pin that one on you, but you sure aren't helping things. No, I don't want to take this outside. Always the macho man, Mark. Big tough Mark, Mr. Tough Guy, you're so sad, man. Oh, I'm the sad one? Well you're sadder. Hey, fuck you! What does my wife have to do with this? Jesus Christ, Mark, you are such a liar. Look what you made me do, I just blasphemed in a church. I don't care if you don't believe in God, Mark, that has nothing to do with any of this. Well I'm sure you'll believe when you are burning in hell. Say one more word, Mark, one more motherfucking word, and I swear to you the cemetery will clear a spot for you, right next to Ray. Yes, yes, you're right, Mark, we're the stupid ones, and you are Mr. Smart. Bye, Mark!

Okay, now that we got that over with, let's remember Ray. Ray was a Morgy. For those of you out there who aren't familiar with the jargon of Ray's industry, that means he played corpses in the motion pictures. Ray did over 40 films in his day. He was amazing, I mean any of the other Morgy's would tell you that. When it came to remaining inanimate for a long period of time Ray was like a praying mantis. Beautiful, man, beautiful. Unfortunately, like all of us who work too much, he started to make little flubs. You could see him breathing. The breathing corpse in The Devil's Own…that was Ray. He had started to blink too, which is never good. Ray was such an overachiever, he just wanted to entertain, and when he started slipping, he took drastic measures. After he was fired from the set of Ilsa's Seduction 3 for breathing, he had his lungs medically removed. The authorities *are* still looking for the doctor. Ray didn't survive long without his lungs. Actually, three minutes was much longer than anyone expected him to live, so there's even more proof of what an amazing guy he was.

The thing is, I think maybe Ray wanted it this way. I mean, this is his ultimate performance right here.

Immaculate. Perfect.

He has certainly convinced all of us that he is dead.

Congratulations, Ray! You're the best, man.

The best.

Precedents

The smell of toilet-brewed sterno fills Cell 5-11 of the LaGrange Penitentiary. Marcia Grable is watching her cell-mate, abusive baby-sitter Tracy Everton, take toxic slugs of the shit-tinged prison moonshine.

Marcia is not at all surprised when Tracy passes out and hits the concrete floor with a wet, fleshy smack. Marcia *is* surprised to find herself laughing, and hard, to the point where her chest aches from it and she feels half crazy. Something about that sound, the loose body slapping the ground, echoes deep inside of her.

It reminds her of the sound of Josh Grable's last moment on Earth.

Back up.

Marcia presses her forehead against the cold window of the prison transit bus and watches the wheat fields roll by until they become a beige blur. She tries to contain the anger that burns holes in her stomach. The handcuffs, secured tight to the seat railing, twist against her wrists and rub her skin red and raw till it throbs.

She remembers the courtroom photograph of Josh's corpse, his lips blue as Arctic glaciers, his hair much lighter than it had been the day before his death.

She tries to feel remorse. She knows it's part of her sentence, but the feeling never comes.

"If they only knew him, if they saw the way he looked at me, with those eyes ...nothing but shark eyes. Just empty. If they knew, I'd be a free woman. If they knew..."

She thinks like this for hours, as her stomach eats itself and bile rises in her throat.

"If they knew my husband like I did, they'd have done the same."

Back up.

The jury foreman reads the sentence so calm you'd think he was reading lawnmower assembly instructions.

Then the monotone voice of the jury foreman drops the word "Guilty" and it hits Marcia's heart sledgehammer-heavy.

A black veil pulls itself over her eyes.

She wakes seconds later, her body tingling as she regains consciousness, hearing her good-for-nothing state appointed lawyer yelling.

"Give her some room, she needs air."

Guilty.

"Fuck air," she thinks, "I need a new lawyer." There is no humor in the thought, only despair on the verge of resignation.

Two days later she steps onto the prison bus and winces as they tighten her handcuffs to the seat railing.

Back up.

Marcia's lawyer is going over the details, the ugly details, during her deposition. He says the state has a very strong case, and they've already secured the librarian and the store clerk to testify. He says the doorknob is an incredibly damaging piece of evidence. The jury will have to know everything, every nasty little detail of her private life, in order to build sympathy for her case.

It's going to be rough, he says. The defense will play up Josh's childhood, with its daily abuses and lingering scars. They'll try to shift the blame back a generation, to Josh's father, Darren. They'll make Marcia the monster and turn Josh into a sympathetically scarred psyche incapable of escaping his childhood hell.

"And the jurors will eat it up, Marcia. This is a jury of your peers. They watch the same TV movies. They belong to Oprah's Book Club. You can take any monster, slap a bad dad into his past, and all of a sudden he's just another lost soul, lashing out. And you were the poor lady that got in the way. They'll argue *you* lacked compassion. You were the one who took things too far."

The defense's plan makes sense to her. She can't even count the number of nights she'd spent trying to blame her own mother for telling her, "Marriage demands compromise." Shifting the blame is so easy. The cheapest freedom she'd ever found. But nothing can justify what Josh did.

"They can't do that. I never even met his father. Everything Josh did, he did of his own free will."

"You talk like that, Marcia, you put that point of view into *your* testimony and you'll kill our case. If we can't blame Josh for what *you* did..."

And her crime, he says, comes across as too calculated.

"I wish you could have committed a simple crime of passion. People who commit crimes of passion often get off with manslaughter. People can sympathize with lover's rage. People can put themselves in that position, they can feel their own finger on the trigger, anxious to squeeze."

Marcia says nothing.

"What you did, Marcia, will not be construed as a crime of passion. Your actions involved too much forethought. We'll be lucky to get a life sentence. You have chosen to commit what will be perceived as a coldhearted murder in a state very fond of capital punishment."

Marcia is staring at the tile floor, agonizing at the thought of airing her family's dirty laundry. Her mind flashes on a syringe full of strychnine, a thumb hovering over the plunger.

"So, where do I begin?"

Back up.

Marcia is at her friend Theresa's house when the police cruiser pulls up.

Her first thought creates a sick panic in her heart.

"I haven't finished cleaning up yet...maybe they're just here to ask questions ...whereabouts...something...oh God... if they've been to the house...oh shit...I haven't fixed the doorknob yet. That fucking doorknob...this is too soon. I was supposed to make the call. So who called? His boss? Was he supposed to work today? Oh, God. Oh, God, he was. Shit, okay, play it straight, ride this out. You were cleaning the house, then you spent the night here. That's it. God, please..."

She has been preparing for this moment, and when the cop breaks the news about Josh's death she shakes and her hands tremble, and the tears well up, and she mutters, "This just can't be."

She had read on the internet that denial was supposed to be her first response.

"This just can't be, officer."

She hopes her nervousness reads as shock. She fights back an incredibly strange urge to smile.

The urge to smile disappears as the handcuffs cut into her wrists.

Back up.

Marcia drives to her friend Theresa's house at four in the morning. She is fighting back laughter, afraid the sound of her own voice would resonate as distant, crazy. She has her windows rolled down, hoping to cleanse herself of the smell.

She drives just two miles over the speed limit, knowing that being pulled over right now would destroy her alibi.

"I'll get to Theresa's and we'll have a cup of tea and we'll watch the sun rise. How long has it been since I've seen the sunrise?"

Too damn long, she concludes, and she laughs, and it does make her feel crazy, but it feels better than being afraid.

Back up.

Marcia opens every window in every room of her small manufactured home. She grabs her keys off the kitchen counter, puts them in her pocket, and then heads back to the bathroom. She picks up the towel pressed tight against the bottom of the door and shuffles away, careful not to inhale deeply until she reaches the kitchen. She grabs a plastic container from beneath the kitchen sink, and carries it, along with the towel, to her backyard, where she has ignited a burn barrel. She drops the items in and watches as they both glow green. Her eyes follow the thick black plumes of swirling smoke as they rise towards the stars.

Back up.

Josh Grable suddenly sounds very sober as he yells, "Marcia, help me out here, let me out of this fucking bathroom or I swear to God..."

His screams are interrupted by violent, retching coughs, and he pounds on the door with enough force that she hears the wood splintering, and just for one second she thinks he may live, and oh God if he gets out of there he's going to torture me, he's going to tear me to pieces, he's going to kill me.

"Please, God," she thinks.

Her prayer is answered by the sound of his body hitting the ground with a wet, fleshy smack as the toilet flushes behind him.

She is confronted by an unexpected surge of tears, sitting cross-legged on the floor, waiting for him to die. Her tears dry quickly as she remembers why this must happen.

She waits for a few minutes to confirm his death, through his silence. Once she feels confident of the fact she cleans up, pulling the duct tape off of the outside of the bathroom window, opening the windows in every room of the house.

"My husband's had a horrible accident," she thinks.

"Thank God."

Back up.

Marcia lies in the dark, feeling Josh's sweat cool on her body. "He drank two bottles. He'll have to piss sooner or later."

She waits—heart beating hummingbird fast in the dark room—hoping he won't pass out.

After twenty minutes he finally rises from the bed and staggers to the bathroom. She pads softly behind him, and when he closes the door she locks it quietly from the outside, and grabs the towel she'd placed in the nearby closet. She pushes the towel as tight as she can between the carpet and the door, knowing her life depends on covering that gap.

She hears his urine splattering against the porcelain, a few spurts and then a long steady stream. She hears him gasp for air, and then he makes a loud gagging noise. She sees the doorknob jiggle, then shake violently. It takes Josh a long, drunken moment to realize the doorknob's been locked from the outside.

Marcia hears his voice, confused, desperate.

"Marsh, wake up! Help me out here!"

"I'm right here, Josh."

"Marsh, I think I'm in trouble here! I can barely breathe! My fuckin' eyes ...oh shit ...aaah ...Marsh, open the door, it's broke or somethin'!"

"No."

"Oh shit, honey, I can't...ah...I...what the fuck is going on here? Open the Goddamned door!"

Silence.

"Marsh ...this isn't funny ...you're gonna ...I mean, is this about the other night ...I'm sorry, Marsh, I'm real sorry about all that ...now quit playing your little games and OPEN THE FUCKING DOOR!"

"Fuck you."

"Marcia, help me out here..."

Back up.

Marcia's day speeds by, and an almost giddy feeling fills her body as she does her shopping. At a Shop Rite she purchases a new lock for the bathroom door; a few tree-shaped air fresheners for her car, three bottles of Sheppard Springs merlot, and a box of Wheat Snacks.

She drives across town to the Home Value wholesalers and makes a few inquiries with a store clerk about cleaning products. She asks about their respective strengths, how concentrated they are, and which ones are really industrial potency. The look on the face of the store clerk says he's never in his entire life seen anyone so excited about cleaning products.

Then Marcia drives home and works frantically, breaking out in cold sweats and hot flashes as she prepares for Josh to come home. She puts a gouge into her left thumb as she replaces the bathroom lock with the new one she purchased. It is the exact same model, but once she finishes installing it, the lock is on the outside.

She then heads into the bathroom and carefully bails out the toilet water currently sitting in the bowl. Cup by cup, she pours it down the sink. She uncaps her Home Value purchase and empties its contents into the bowl. The smell is so strong she recoils. It feels like a butane torch burning inside of her lungs, so she exits quickly and leaves the door just a tiny crack open.

By the time Josh gets home and takes off his Berwood Mall Security outfit she's already got a bottle of red wine cracked and she nearly pours it down his throat and kisses his neck and tells him she wants it to be like old times, she wants to party and so they party and skip dinner and she drinks one bottle and he sucks down the other two and then he pulls her into the bedroom and he's rubbing his crotch and mumbling to himself and she's nervous cause he's looking at her with those empty shark eyes and she doesn't want to get hurt so she goes to him and he smashes himself into her and pushes down on top of her but he's so drunk he can't get it in and he tries and he wraps his arms around her and squeezes hard, too hard and she can't breathe, and she starts to panic and he looks in her eyes like he wants to just crush her away into nothing and sweat drips from his forehead onto her face and he suddenly gives and rolls off of her and they lie there.

Marcia hates him more than ever.

Eventually he rises and stumbles to the bathroom.

Back up.

The librarian was very helpful, and showed Marcia how to use the internet properly, how to hold the mouse and enter keywords like "grieving process."

The computer, intended for public use, records every page Marcia visits.

The page that talks about safety and cleaning products.

The page that teaches her the cogeners in red wines and dark alcoholic beverages increase the level of ammonia in urine.

The page about dealing with the loss of a loved one.

Marcia makes an impression.

Back up.

Theresa opens the door to her house and finds Marcia sobbing on her stoop.

Minutes later, after Marcia tells her story, Theresa makes a suggestion. Theresa says, "A man like that deserves to fucking die. I see this sort of thing on TV all the time. Drunken husband, abused wife. A lot of these wives, even if they leave, they're the ones that end up dead."

She then proceeds to make other suggestions, talking up counseling and police intervention. It doesn't matter, because inside Marcia's head she hears Theresa saying, over and over again, "A man like that deserves to fucking die." These words echo deep. They set into her bones, take hold behind her eyes.

Theresa makes an impression.

Back up.

Marcia sits on the toilet, weeping, holding her bruised back and her belly.

The water in the toilet beneath her is dark crimson.

Her mind is sick with pain, trembling in her head as she thinks, "Oh, God, please let me have him back, please let me have Hollis back, I swear I'm sorry for whatever I've done that made this happen, I swear, God please let me have him back, he wasn't even born and I would have loved him so good, and he would have loved me back, and loved me, nobody loves me, please God..."

She sits there for two hours as the water beneath her grows darker and her skin grows cold.

Back up.

She is asleep and doesn't want to wake up. Josh comes home late and rotten with booze. He tries to crawl on top of her and she pushes him back.

His eyes change.

He changes. He leaves his heart in the space behind him and moves forward like a machine. He makes fists, his knuckles crack.

She curls up in a ball and lets him hit her until he collapses, like he always does.

He grunts and hisses out breath hot with alcohol as his hands crunch into her body.

He doesn't know she's six weeks late for her period.

He falls asleep with his knuckles purple, and doesn't wake as Marcia crawls to the bathroom.

Back up.

Marcia is fifteen, and pays very close attention to her Home Ec. teacher when he emphasizes the danger of mixing ammonia and bleach when cleaning your house.

"They call it chlorine gas, people, and it killed thousands in World War I. Don't let it kill you because you're not paying attention."

The lesson makes an impression.

Back up.

Marcia is five and asks her Mom what she dreamed of being when she grew up. Her mom says, "I just wanted to have a beautiful baby and a kind husband to take care of and love. That's all I ever wanted, really."

Marcia agrees that it's about the loveliest dream she's ever heard.

Working At Home

A needle sharp moment of pain in Dr. Frank Challing's ankle distracts him for less than a second, and is easily brushed off. His brain is otherwise occupied, a maelstrom of activity as he learns that his memories of the day's events won't wipe clean, no matter how hard he tries to ignore or deny them. He attempts to keep his brain free of thought through labor. He sweeps, mops, scrubs, polishes, and drips salt sweat from his slick forehead as he compulsively brings the entire kitchen to a smooth luster.

His hard work fails in the face of his memory, and every time his eyelids close he can see the nightmare in full color.

The girl is there, torn to tatters.

The strange doctors are there, holding him, watching her, waiting for the things to finish eating.

Mr. Devries had told him, "You mustn't think too deeply about it, Frank."

Mr. Devries hadn't been present at the phlebotomy lab today, and had no idea how impossible executing his recommendation would be. Mr. Devries didn't have to throw his clothes in the incinerator today. Mr. Devries did not spend three hours in quarantine. Mr. Devries had not had to watch *them.*

Frank is suddenly wracked with shudders and a greasy cold sweat.

He looks in desperation around the kitchen and finds it in immaculate status, clean enough to satisfy a legion of anal-retentive Martha Stewart acolytes. It takes him three seconds to reach the liquor cabinet. It is the first time he has ever felt like he lunged for something, and it shocks him. He grabs a bottle of Hennessey but does not bother to look through the cabinet for his favorite snifter, the one he got in his High Roller's Suite at Luxor.

A rapid twist of his left thumb sends the cap of the bottle plunging to the floor, making a plastic click as it strikes the ground. The first slug goes back like water, as does the second, and it's only on the fifth gulp that he feels flush, his skin tingling. Frank almost makes a tight face in reaction to the gasoline burn in his belly and throat, but restrains himself. He has always seen the post-liquor cringe as a sign of weakness and lack of personal control.

You and your control, Frank! Just live for once.

He hasn't heard the real thing in three years, but his ex-wife's voice still gets on his nerves from time to time.

Oh, so you won't talk to me about your work, huh? You sure don't mind talking to that bottle.

"She was always so damned dramatic," Frank thinks as he walks into his entertainment room and sets the bottle of cognac on the coffee table in front of him. He hangs his head and sighs. The sigh is stertorous and thick, and to Frank's discomfort, more than a little shaky. "Jesus, calm down!" He can hear the slight electric hum of his refrigerator in the kitchen, and it makes him uneasy.

It is quiet enough for him to think.

I don't even know what her name was. She never said anything. All she could do was scream while those things...

Frank's thoughts are interrupted by a sound he does not recognize. He picks up his bottle of cognac and walks toward the sound coming from the bay windows on the far west side of his loft.

"Is someone humming in here?" His feet tread softly across the cold floor as he approaches his windows. As he nears the edge of his loft a gust of wind speeds across the black-tinted surface of the bay windows, howling first, then reducing to a high-pitched whisper.

"The wind must be blowing sixty miles an hour out there. It's making my damn windows vibrate," he thinks. "Could the pressure suck my windows out of the building?"

He pictures himself sucked out with the windows, twisting like a leaf in the screaming winds until he and the glass panels hit the pavement at the same time. Rough cleanup. He shivers again.

Frank takes his ninth and tenth gulps off the bottle, which has grown significantly lighter. This sensation of decreased weight barely registers in his mind. Frank also pays little notice to the slight itch on his inner right ankle as it turns into a burning sensation. Frank is too buzzed to notice the small but spreading red spot on the side of his white Avia sock.

He sees a blinking red light in the corner of his left eye, and feels for a moment that he may pass out. He grabs onto a decorative Japanese hutch and steadies himself, lets the blood flow back into his head. "Thought I was about to go down. Better slow up on this shit." He sets the bottle down hard on the hutch.

As he revolves his head his sight takes a moment to catch up with the movement and then whips into position, arriving in his eyes with a liquid slosh, the effect of which is nauseating. He still sees the blinking red light out of his peripheral, and then realizes it's his answering machine. Blink, blink, pause: two messages.

His finger presses in the dust free plastic button marked "Play" and there are a few seconds of analog sounding hiss. At first he does not recognize the voice, and thinks it might be one of those damn telemarketers. Then, with a degree of shame, he realizes it is his daughter's voice.

"Hello...well, I hope I'm leaving this message in the right place 'cause there was no greeting or anything, your machine just beeps. Anyway, this message is for Frank Challing, and if I've got the right machine, then Hi, Dad! First of all I have to say I missed you at the wedding, and I totally disagree with Mom's politics on this...she's just...well, you know Mom. Enough of that, I just wanted to say thank you for the gift, Mark and I had a fabulous time in Nagano, and the skiing was absolutely gorgeous. S ...thank you. Mom wouldn't give me your new phone number, she's burning bridges left and right, so I found you on the internet. This call cost me twenty bucks! Kidding! I just had to call, I miss you and I had this dream...I don't know...I just...never mind, now I feel kind of stupid. Anyway, again, thank you, and I miss you and love you! I can't wait to see you again, Daddy! You owe me a hug. My number and my address are still the same. Call me."

Frank, with one hand against the wall for balance, says, "I love you too, honey..." He feels grateful for her call. As another torrent of wind shakes the windows to his right he thinks, "Hell, I'm overjoyed if the phone company calls these days." Before Frank can feel a moment of the self-pity which he loathes and sees approaching, the second message starts.

"Francis, it's Devries. You must get a message on that machine of yours. I apologize for calling this time of the evening, but I must clarify a few things about today's incident for you. Listen very carefully; this is a matter of utmost security. Top brass at the hospital have decided to let you know certain things about both the patient and the illness that afflicted her. We will be sending an escort to your residence at seven tomorrow morning. You will accompany him to the hospital and receive full disclosure of the facts in this case. In the meantime, I must demand that you do not speak to anyone in regards to this matter, even your family. To do so could mean the endangerment of both your position at our facility and the security of the facility itself. You may be aware of the financial backing we've been receiving from a third party in certain areas of research. I don't feel anything else needs to be said. I will see you in the morning, Frank. Have a pleasant evening, and enjoy the storm. It should be quite dramatic."

Frank finds the whole message incredulous, and anger grows in his alcohol-filled belly. He notices the strange lack of urgency in Devries' voice, and wonders why he hadn't said all this when he talked to Frank at his locker after quarantine earlier in the evening. "What's all this shit about outside funding? And 'Have a pleasant evening'? That asshole. He can't just write off what that girl had as an *illness*!"

He remembers the way the girl had dived into his phlebotomy lab, her ropy veins extended to their limit all over her body, blood pressure obviously soaring. She crashed into Frank, and rushed back to the corner of his office as two doctors in scrub colors he didn't recognize came in through his door and closed it behind them.

As the girl passed Frank he smelled blood, an electric, copper penny smell, and a deeper, earthier smell, like damp topsoil. The intruding doctor with the dark hair said something like, "Please step back, sir." but Frank was too mesmerized by the girl in the corner to hear the request.

She was tearing herself apart. Her fingernails sank into the skin of her belly and tore upwards, leaving dark rivulets of torn matter. Her eyes were full of abject terror, and didn't seem to focus on anything, just flitted from left to right, up and down. They made contact with Frank's eyes for one second, and were full of pleading. Her eyes were screaming HELP ME! and Frank stepped forward to and was yanked back and placed in a stranglehold by the shorter intruding doctor. "Sir, you do not want to approach the patient. She is incredibly dangerous," said the strange doctor as his bicep flexed tighter into Frank's trachea.

Frank wanted so desperately to break free and help the girl, and he was attempting to shake loose and demand the two men help him when *it* happened. The young girl screamed, "THEY'RE INSIDE OF ME. GET THEM OUT! GET THEM OUT!" and was struck by some kind of seizure that flopped her back onto the floor, her head striking first and making a thick thud on the cold tile. Her back arched tight and blood bubbled from her mouth, running down the sides of her face, which then smeared with her sweat as she swung her head from left to right. As she arched her body her gown flopped back on to her face and muffled the gargling noises and panic filled grunts that her body forced out as she hemorrhaged. She managed to scream, "GET THEM OUT!" again and Frank had never been so afraid as when he saw what she was referring to.

He saw them then, hundreds of them, some kind of worm or parasite, snaking around just beneath the surface of her waxy white skin. She was seething with them. It looked like every inch of her body was crawling across her frame, all of her flesh in motion, and then Frank heard the sound, the sick tearing sound, and realized they were eating her, her connective tissues. These worm things were skinning her from the inside, eating everything that held her together, and Frank felt a sudden urge to vomit, and a stronger urge to run from the room, but he was still held tight by the man in the strange orange scrubs. Frank watched—the girl's skin grew loose as if she had aged a hundred years in ten seconds, the flesh of her face now slack and drooping anywhere the worms weren't moving beneath it.

She stilled and her back stopped arching and slapped wet to the tile and Frank thought that she was dead then but her body kept moving, shifting and bulging with the rapid snaking motions of the worms. One of her eyes, unencumbered by her drooping eyelids, pushed out onto her cheek, and Frank saw a mottled gray and pink worm slide out onto her face via the new hole.

The doctor guarding the door spoke in an almost jovial tone. "Rough cleanup, huh, Andolini?" He then stepped forward and pulled a spray bottle from a green pack that Frank hadn't noticed him carrying. He looked at Frank from the corner of his eye, never taking his sights off the twitching, boiling infestation on the floor. "Andolini, get that guy out of here. She's about to split."

As two rough hands pulled him from the room Frank saw the other doctor poised with his sleek aluminum spray can over the dead girl on the floor. She was bleeding from every orifice, and her skin began to tear open in hundreds of places, little gray and pink segmented worms spilling out, blood-slick. Frank was jerked roughly into the hallway and heard the doctor still inside mutter, "Dear God..."

What the hell is going on?

It's Frank's ex-wife's voice again, inside his head, and he resents the intrusion, but his rapid heartbeat and drunken confusion echo the sentiment. The contents of the day hit Frank with a unified impact, and his mind flashes over everything at once, his job, his loneliness, him nearly crying when he heard his daughter's voice, his ridiculous cleaning routine, his spontaneous liquor binge, the doctors in the orange scrubs saying "rough cleanup," and the girl, that poor girl being eaten alive from the inside. He had kept quiet about it, and just rolled right through quarantine without asking a single question, half of him feeling catatonic, the other half trapped in terror-induced denial. He tried to take Devries' suggestion and not think too deeply about it, but he had watched those worms skin a girl *inside* in just a few minutes, and he didn't help her, he *couldn't help her...*

You could have helped her, Frank. You were afraid. So you watched her die and then you kept quiet about it for no good reason, and now you're diving into a bottle of booze. You wonder why we got divorced? Look at you. You're not a man.

Desperate to flush the voice out of his head, Frank turns away from the answering machine and makes a rush for the bottle sitting on the hutch. As he takes his second step forward he feels a strange, warm *shift* in his right ankle, followed by a pain so sharp he almost falls over from the white hot shock of it.

"What in Christ's name did I do there? I must have stepped on my foot at the wrong angle. My fault for staggering around like this," he thinks and he takes another step forward. He steps with care and as his right foot hits the carpet his ankle explodes in pain. Focus blurs until everything around him looks like it's underwater and he falls to the ground, almost unconscious from the razor-sharp agony in his ankle. He cries out to the empty apartment and feels almost instantly embarrassed, somewhere past the immediacy of the pain. He gingerly pulls his right ankle in towards himself as he sits with his left leg splayed. He pulls back the cuff of his pant leg and expects another surge of pain. Instead he finds his sock soaking wet with blood.

"I'm bleeding. I'm *bleeding*. What the hell did I do to myself here?" he thinks, and as he reaches down and grabs the edge of his sock he prepares for the worst. The lights in his apartment flicker for a moment, throwing a tiny strobe effect on the floor that Frank mistakes for a drunken hallucination. He starts to roll back the fabric of his sock, which is now saturated with dark blood, and as he nears the base of his ankle he is struck by another shockwave of pain, this one strong enough to floor him. He flops back, unconscious as his head strikes the carpet with a muffled thud. As the wave of pain washes over and through and out of Frank he regains consciousness and feels a primal tingle in his extremities. He sits up slowly and waits for his pixelated vision to orient. For a moment he doesn't know where he is or how he got into his position.

The apartment is now pitch black.

Frank feels like he's at the bottom of a swimming pool filled with India ink. He can hardly breathe and his forehead is beaded with sweat. He hears another gust of wind whip through the street outside and realizes the storm must have knocked the power out. The thin crescent moon above sheds no light into skyscraper apartments, unless you have a penthouse.

"Great, just great! I got drunk, somehow broke my ankle, and now I'm blind," he thinks, with little humor. His heartbeat picks up as he surveys the situation. "I've got to get to my flashlight and see exactly what's going on with my ankle."

Frank orients himself in the murk and pulls himself over toward a small utility closet near his kitchen. He gasps and grinds his teeth as he feels another *shift* in his ankle, this one up higher than the last. "Why would the pain be moving up my damn leg?" he wonders, and the answer his subconscious formulates makes his heart run at hummingbird speed.

Think about it, Franky Boy.

He feels the strange shift again and braces himself against another wave of pain, digging his elbows hard into the floor, clenching his abdominal muscles, and when he is content the pain has subsided he continues crawling towards the closet. Once there he pulls the thin door open and reaches into the back of the closet and grabs a bag containing his camping equipment. He digs into his neon orange duffle bag and pulls out most of the contents. At the very bottom he finds what he is looking for. He clicks the small rubber button and his Maglite glows bright on the camping debris around him. A parka, a butane torch, two pieces of Readystart kindling, an unfrozen packet of Blue Ice, a small hatchet, a wooly knit hat, a bungee cord, and a large First Aid kit.

He swings the light onto his ankle and very carefully pulls his foot in closer to his groin. His ankle is burning now and he winces as he pulls the cuff of his pant leg back. His sock is sodden with blood. Frank's stomach curls over on itself and threatens to divest itself of its contents. Frank has been living with blood, often sixty hours a week, at the lab, but the sight of his own still makes him feel very small and fragile. He grimaces and pulls the sock back, expecting to see a jutting shard of bone sticking out, figuring a compound fracture would be the only thing that could hurt this much.

Just beneath his inner right ankle, oozing blood, is a perfectly round hole, about the circumference of a pencil. Frank's heart squeezes tight and doesn't release for three seconds, and he struggles, gasping to pull in fresh air. "Now how do I manage to get a puncture wound and not feel it for so long?" he says. Speaking out loud doesn't provide the comfort that he thought it would.

Open your eyes, Franky boy. You brought your work home with you.

That was the phrase Frank's wife used at the divorce hearing. "He brings his work home with him, your Honor. He internalizes all his work stress and brings it home with him and my daughter and I have to deal with his mood swings and tantrums...No, he's never threatened either of us, your Honor, but you should see the look in his eyes after a long shift...No, he seldom has time for myself or my daughter... Yes, sir, he was a stable provider, but if that was all I wanted I would have married Amish." Frank had been stunned when the judge laughed aloud. "Yes, sir, he just values his job more than he values his family."

Frank sits on the floor in a state of disbelief, wondering how the hell he got to exactly where he is now. He knows that thinking about his divorce is morbid and pointless but he is growing more horrified by the second as he looks at the *too perfect* hole in his ankle, and he finds sadness somehow more comforting than terror.

He can barely get his hands to stop shaking long enough to unclasp the metal latch on the old First Aid kit. He opens the box and pulls out a few swabs, a small bottle of alcohol, a pair of scissors, a gauze pad, and a scalpel co-opted from his graduation at Penn State. He holds the Maglite in his mouth, and his breath rolls out rapidly around its metal base, hot and stale. He shifts his body to the right so that his leg rests on the tiled kitchen flooring, and he pulls the plastic parka underneath it to keep the blood from staining the ground.

His teeth press tight against the flashlight, almost to the point of chipping, as he wets a swab with alcohol and prepares to clean the wound. "Hold on," he thinks as he pushes the swab down around the bleeding hole. The sting is instant, but nowhere near the sudden shock he feels when he sees motion beneath his skin. He thinks it is a vein at first, shifting as his foot moves, but then he realizes that no vein wraps around the ankle in a perfect circle.

There, beneath his skin, pulsing to a separate beat than Frank's veins, is a small protrusion. The skin circling his ankle is loose and something thick and warm is moving slowly under the surface.

Frank is sitting still but nearly vomits as his stomach takes a roller-coaster-sized drop. He blinks to clear his sight, and moves the flashlight in closer. There is no doubt. Something foreign is under Frank's skin, and it is making progress up his leg.

He hears the girl screaming.

GET THEM OUT!

Frank panics, heart racing, and strips off his shirt to check out his skin. His hands rush over the surface, crawl over his face, and he points the Maglite where he can, and he wonders how many are inside of him, right now, chewing away at the things that hold him together, unstitching him, eating him. He pulls his shoes off and throws them over his shoulders. One of them topples a glass vase with some old dried flowers in it, and it shatters as it strikes the floor. Frank barely notices. His panic becomes overwhelming as he strips off his socks and checks his feet.

"If there were any more of those things in me right now I'd feel them," he hopes, thinking of the intense pain that this one small visitor is causing him.

There is another shift as the warm, soft intruder begins to move up towards Frank's calf, and the pain hits him in the belly, and Frank turns his head to the left. This time he can't hold back and the night's booze gushes out of his mouth, the Maglite falling to the floor with the deluge. "Whatever this thing is doing under my skin, it's toxic." His heaving subsides.

Do something, Franky boy.

A bolt of adrenaline singes Frank's nerves and he finds himself very anxious to get this *thing* out of his body before another wave of that sick gutfire pain hits. He remembers seeing the girl tearing away at herself with her own hands.

Oriented by the adrenaline, Frank decides to proceed in a more civilized manner.

He reaches down and picks up the alcohol swab and the scalpel and turns to his left and picks up the wet Maglite and puts it back between his teeth. He brings his right leg close again and swabs the area just above the intruder, and as he brings the scalpel closer he wishes both that he had never drank that evening and that he were much more drunk.

The paradox of self-surgery, Franky. How do you stay alert and steady while anesthetized? Can you, Franky? Can you even do this? You couldn't save our marriage, can you save your own life?

Frank feels like yelling "Shut up, you bitch!" but realizes there's no one in the apartment but him.

The slow pulsing movement of the parasite chewing its way up the inside of Frank's leg pulls him back into focus and he pushes the scalpel into the skin just above the worm's path. Flooded with endorphins, Frank barely feels the metal blade slice into his skin, creating a ten centimeter wide cut through every layer. He sits and stares, repulsed as the worm moves closer to the hole, intent on its path. Sweat drips from Frank's forehead as he reaches over and grabs a cheap, tarnished pair of tweezers from the First Aid kit. He sees a tiny movement in the wound he has spread open and watches as the worm's head comes into view. It is grayish pink in the few spots that aren't slick with blood, and at the head, where Frank expects to see tiny, razor sharp teeth, he instead sees a thin white mucus being secreted from the mouth of the worm. Frank has never heard of a parasite that actively melts its host's tissues with a secreted acid, and he's watched a lot of Discovery since the divorce.

"Someone made this. Why in the hell would someone make this?" he thinks and is fascinated and disgusted at the same time as he moves the tweezers in towards the head of the worm.

The worm seems to sense the tweezers as they approach, and it retracts itself a bit, the motion sending bolts of pain through Frank's leg, like white phosphor burning under his skin. He seizes on the pain and pushes the tweezers in deep and clasps them down when he finds purchase. He has the tweezers an inch deep into the wound and they are clamped tight around the soft body of the worm.

The worm ruptures.

Frank swiftly pulls the tweezers out to discover they are holding onto only half of the worm, its thick gray pink segment still twisting above the metal. He pulls the segment closer to the flashlight and has to look at it almost cross-eyed to focus. Then he sees the nature of the parasite.

"This is how I am going to die."

Inside the twisting segment clasped in the tweezers, just beneath the near translucent skin of the worm, Frank sees *them*. The babies. The thousands of tiny worms inside the larger one. The big one's just their mother, the delivery system.

He can feel them, the army of tiny worms squirming loose from the torn carcass of the large one, and he realizes that this is what happened to the girl. They get under your skin, find a nice place to rest, and then they burst, and the thousands of newborns tear you to pieces, inside.

He internalizes his work, your Honor.

Frank feels a moment of nothing. He has never felt so empty and alone, hopeless and ready to die. Then, as the pain in his leg starts to spread like quicksilver, two sentences echo in his head, spurring him to action. He hears the voices of two girls.

The first voice screams, the sound of the violated.

"GET THEM OUT OF ME!"

The second voice speaks, the sound of love.

"I can't wait to see you again, Daddy!"

Driven by an animal-level desire to survive, Frank reaches for the kindling hatchet that he had pulled out of his camping bag. He sits there, watching his leg seethe and squirm beneath the surface, and hesitates for one second before bringing the blade down on his leg just above the knee.

The first swing of the blade flays his leg wide open, exposing subcutaneous fat and the meat of his muscle. The second swing strikes marrow, and for a second the blade hesitates to release from his femur as he jerks it back up for another blow. The third swing shatters bone and tears all the way through his leg. The blade sticks into the floor beneath him.

He grabs the wooly knit hat in one hand and the butane torch in the other and pushes himself ten feet away from the remainder of his right leg, leaving a thick gout of blood behind him. He presses the cap onto the stump and tries to staunch the flow from his vast wound. He is close to shock and his blood pressure dips dangerously low as he ignites the butane torch. Acting on his last reserves he pulls the soaking wooly knit hat off of the stump and turns the butane torch to the wound, knowing that he's more likely to survive a third degree burn than total blood loss.

He has never known such pain. His body is overcome with throbbing, absolute pain, pure as fire, and he stays in motion only by will and adrenaline.

He has never felt so alive as he does in each moment of this that he survives.

He drags himself over to the twitching, decimated leg in the kitchen and places the flame of the butane torch to the hive that was once part of his body, setting his Readystart kindling on each side of it.

As he watches the leg burn down to the blackened tile and hears the soft boiling sound of the worms bursting he feels shock settle in. He thinks, "Mr. Devries, I hereby tender my resignation," and doesn't recognize the sound of his own voice, laughing.

Frank wants to live and does what he can to survive. He tries to care for his wound as he prepares to leave the smoky apartment. A small blanket off the back of his couch is wrapped around his stump and secured triple tight by a bungee cord acting as a makeshift tourniquet. A handful of Vicodin allow him to move in spite of the crippling pain. A varnished cypress walking stick with an ornate lion's head handle keeps him from toppling.

As he leaves his apartment he grabs his hatchet, wipes it clean, and tucks it into the waist of his pants. He also collects his keys, his wallet, his hidden stash of large bills totaling four thousand dollars, and a small note with an address and phone number.

He carries the hatchet in case the escort Mr. Devries mentioned is waiting outside of his building. Mr. Devries, who wanted Frank to keep quiet. Mr. Devries, who had access to Frank's locker, and knew about the parasites. Mr. Devries, who hadn't been worried about Frank talking to anyone because he didn't expect Frank to see the dawn of the next day.

He carries the cash so he can bribe the first taxi driver he can find in the aftermath of the storm to take him to a hospital three counties away, where Mr. Devries can't find him, at least not right away.

He carries the note so he can call his daughter from the hospital and tell her he has some unexpected time off from work.

Priapism

I really think this lecture is warranted, Ron. Actually, don't think of it as a lecture. Let's not set up some sort of teacher/student dynamic, when it's both of us who should be learning from what you have been doing. I mean, I know exactly what I'm talking about here, so I suppose I'm not actually learning anything, but I just don't want you to think I'm condescending you. I have always tried to treat you as an equal Ron, regardless of our age difference and familial relationship. On the inside you have an intellect, and while it may not be as finely honed as mine, it must be respected. Intellect must be worshipped, Ron. It, and the opposable thumb, and maybe nuclear power, are the only things that save us from spending all day crawling about in the woods, foraging for berries and biting into boars with our little incisors.

Consider that a rhesus monkey one third my weight has muscles that are five times stronger. It's my intellect versus his muscles. Look who won, Ronny! Of course our intellect saved us. The rhesus monkey is now relegated to carnival work, and in some cases, the care of quadriplegics. How's that for the victory of the mind? A little cerebellum in the skull and you can make vicious, fetid animals serve and wipe the asses of invalids.

I'm trying to establish a respect in you, a respect for the power, the immense force that your mind can wield. As I was saying, even when you were in your crib, mewling and shitting your plastic diapers, I respected the mind that I knew you had. I read to you each night, fine works by Plato, and

Pynchon, and Joyce, and I think maybe you understood. You had a look in your eyes when I was reading to you, although it was always post your evening breast feeding, so that look may have just been a symptom of gas. Or perhaps, as I believe, it was a combination of gas and understanding. Yes, that was it. You were tiny, but your mind was stewing to a head as swiftly as your bowels.

Oh, forgive my scatological way of speaking. I suppose by speaking as such I only hurt the thoughts and ideas I wish to serve. Ron, you must learn that ideas can be greater than the man who thinks them. Ideas are the finery we wrap our brains in, to hide the reptile core that we can't escape. The reptile brain, Ron, is a vestige of the past from which we can't seem to slip loose. We chug-chug-chug toward the future, and the world of ideas grows exponentially, but we are still base creatures at times. We all have those sad, tragic moments where we neglect thought and act on old, withered snippets of instinct.

Ron, never respect instinct. Look where instincts got the manatees. Every year, without thinking, they return to the same waters so they can be Ginsued to bloody shreds by my new outboard Yamaha motor. You remember how we always used to go to Florida? Killing those manatees was not just good fun, it was a statement, a bright red example of the superiority of man's intellect. It's a seamless statement really. There I am, with my loving nuclear family, sitting in a creation of man's genius, of man's hard work, and will, and intellect. Thanks to the mind, Ron, we were capable of attaining great speeds over an environment which humans have always found threatening, and as a result of our actions, those creatures controlled by instinct, by mechanical synaptic triggers, incapable of truly thinking, incapable of writing an immaculate Haiku, incapable of speaking five languages, those dull creatures were destroyed.

We survived, we enjoyed and consumed. We Goddamn transcended! We were in control!

Ron, you know your Dad can be a little passionate about things of this nature.

Right there, right there, that's it though, Ron. That duplicitous mixture of physical passion and intellect, that's where you have try to keep yourself. That's where the genius comes from. Like Beethoven, he had the intellect, but until he felt the wave of beats and sound against his head, with his head on the piano, that's when the genius happened. That mixture, Ron, once felt, is something you can really believe in. Then you search for it, and the more you search for it, the closer you get to the brilliance of yourself.

Ron, we really do need to address what you have been doing. Your mother recently brought to my attention that you have been violating yourself.

Masturbation, Ron.

Now I can see by the blood in your cheeks that this is true. I had hoped that your mother was misled, but now there's no doubt. Ron, you are fourteen, so I don't expect you to be engaging in sexual relations yet, and I'm certain you feel certain needs, but there has to be a better way of expressing those desires. Masturbation has nothing to do with thought, Ron, absolutely nothing to do with the intellect that I have tried to instill in you. It is a simple case of stimulus and response. Oh, I'm certain the mind comes into play at times, when your body needs some sort of stimulus maybe the mind has to create a fantasy, but that sort of thing doesn't really count.

Worse yet, your mother has had to clean up for your filthy behavior. Your effluvia have managed to clog up the shower twice, and while in a certain way I can admire your raw physical tenacity, this is really just disgusting. Not thoughtful at all. Great men do not jerk off, son. Great men take that sexual tension which is now budding inside of you, and they control it. They subvert it.

Try to look at any great achievement of man and not find repressed sex, sublimated wants and needs. Pyramids, the "breasts" of mother Egypt, the music of Strauss, rife with sweat and lust, and look at skyscrapers for God's sake. Nothing is a more obvious phallus than a skyscraper. That no architect ever had the honesty to attach some sort of testes to his building surprises me.

So, Ron, I need you to stop defiling yourself as soon as possible, and stay out of our room especially. Your mother's high heels are never to be touched again!

You must be wondering what your punishment is Ronald. I don't always see justice in parental punishment, and I would prefer to think that we could simply confer, mind to mind, and that would be that, but in this case, when your behavior involves such a gut-wrenchingly simian action, I feel that the punishment needs to be more direct, more Skinneresque. And I cannot forget the immense effectiveness of my father's own methods, upon discovering me with one of his cigars. Smoking the lot nearly killed me, but I learned, damn it. I learned.

So, young man, now the time is at hand, pardon my dubious pun.

You are going to masturbate non-stop for the next five hours, while I play the complete works of Kenny Loggins on your mother's piano. I can't think of any music less erotic. You will have no lubricant; you will have no stimulating reading materials. You will not be allowed near any shoes. You are to go over into that bare corner and sit on the rough wooden floor, and you are to whack it for an immense duration of time. If your penis becomes flaccid, you must continue pumping. If you begin to bleed, then you may have a styptic pencil for sealing the wound, but this is the only concession I will grant you. Whenever you have an orgasm you must pray to your own intellect to forgive you. You must say to your mind, "I am sorry for being a dirty ape!" At the end of these five hours you will be put directly to sleep, regardless of the loss of fluids, proteins, and electrolytes. When you awake in the morning you may have sore genitals and extreme forearm fatigue, but you will be a better, brighter person. Perhaps you will even become a man. It can happen just like that, when you finally take control of your mind and your life.

I am going to grab some vermouth and my Kenny Loggins sheet music, and I think you should get into the corner right now. I will let you know as soon as I am ready to begin your healing. Tomorrow, Ron, you'll thank me for this, but for now we begin our descent into the beast.

Whip it out, son; it is time to make some repairs to your mind.

Two Cages, One Moon

Karen had finally found a level of comfort in the trunk when Steven slowed the car and brought it to a rumbling stop. She had been so comfortable that the empty motor oil container lodged into her lower back didn't hurt anymore and had become a dull presence. In contrast, the handcuffs that bound her were still causing discomfort, as they always did. "Nine months in these damn things and they still hurt."

She heard him rounding the car, coming to the rear with his keys jingling. She sucked down fresh air as he opened the trunk, knowing she wouldn't be out of the stale prison for long.

She was grateful that he took her out for bathroom breaks, even if it was at his convenience. Within the first month after he abducted her from her studio apartment in Boise he had learned it was best to let her out every three or four hours. For practical reasons Karen now received less water and food than she used to. The urine smell had been heavy and floated from the trunk through the upholstery and eventually to Steven's nose whenever she emptied her bladder as a desperate measure. Steven had tried putting her in adult diapers, but Karen had developed a nasty rash and he hadn't like the way it looked or smelled. So, every three or four hours, if there happened to be a rest stop or gas station with bathrooms in the rear he pulled over and let her out for a few minutes. Karen felt Steven's arms sliding under her back and the crook of her legs. He picked her up, grunting, and set her on the ground.

There wasn't anyone else at the rest stop. Karen thought Steven was very good at this, at keeping her, and he never stopped if there was someone who could spot them and see what he was up to. He was desperate to have her, to own her, and somewhere at the back of her head she enjoyed his need.

She held her hands out in front of her. It was part of their ritual. He inserted the tiny silver key and twisted it. He unlatched the cuffs and let her hands loose, knowing she wouldn't strike him or try to run. She had learned her lessons.

The first lesson was "Don't try to run." A blow to her head with his pistol had taught her this.

The second lesson was "Don't scream for help." A fist to her mouth had taught her this. Steven kept the two teeth she had spit out in his right pants pocket.

The third lesson was "Don't fight back." The thick razor scars in the webbing between her fingers had taught her this.

She was docile now, soft as a lamb. She had given up hope of escape after the first brutal week of her abduction.

He didn't hurt her anymore, not like he used to. She found she didn't fear him much, after a while. When he did hurt her it was usually quick and she found she was able to block out most of the pain. Her suffering, like any day-in, day-out routine, now bored her.

The full moons of each month still brought trouble, but other than that their relationship had become strangely placid.

Karen walked into the restroom. She enjoyed it as an oasis from the dark of her mobile prison. It was the only time she was ever alone, physically. Steven was waiting right outside the door for her, with the pistol tucked into the back of his pants, so she never felt free, but being out of the trunk and away from Steven for a few minutes was something she had grown to cherish.

She entered the stall and latched the door shut behind her. She dropped her underwear, the new, poorly fitting underwear that Steven had purchased a few weeks ago, and rested on the cool porcelain with her elbows on her knees and her face cupped in her hands.

Karen saw the lipstick on the ground after she flushed, and until she grasped it she was sure it was a tiny mirage.

She thought for a moment about the content of her days with Steven. She thought about the beatings, and the trunk, the hot trunk full of stale air and rotten smells, and the dehydration, and the way that Steven would try to have sex with her and then hit her when he couldn't get hard, and she felt the anger in her belly turning to fire. She thought about the approaching full moon and wondered how many more cycles she could survive. She seized upon her chance and started writing with the lipstick on the beige wall of the bathroom stall.

She knew Steven would be getting impatient, and when he got nervous he got rough with her, so she acted swiftly, scrawling, "Help! Kidnapped! His name is Steven! We are in a burgundy Impala! Not a joke!"

She wanted to write more but the waxy lipstick ran out before she could get her name on the wall. She tried to lift some excess lipstick from the message with her fingertips, but it began to smear beneath her shaking hands, and she gave up. She was a victim with no name, easier to forget and ignore.

Karen tried to act cool as she exited the bathroom. She had cleaned the makeup from her fingers and wrapped the lipstick container in half a roll of toilet paper and thrown it in the trash. She prayed Steven hadn't grown suspicious.

If he went into the bathroom and checked the stall, what then? She didn't believe he'd kill her. He needed her too much. Still, he could be cruel, and she didn't want to learn any more lessons at the edge of his razor.

She found Steven outside the door, looking at the palm of his hand where her two previously punched-out teeth rested. He was looking at them with adoration. Love.

Karen held out her hands and felt the steel of the handcuffs bite into her raw, chafed wrists.

The next week passed quickly for Karen. She spent most of her time in darkness, cradled in the trunk of the car, sweating and sleeping, stirring through fever dreams. She didn't know what state they were in, but the air in the trunk smelled like onions. She didn't know what month it was, but she knew a full moon must be approaching because Steven was very agitated.

A few months back Steven told Karen that the spirits he trapped in his blood chewed on his insides during a full moon. Steven was weird like that. Karen was fascinated by just how broken and disjointed his mind was, and often sympathized with him even though she didn't know how he had become so twisted up inside. There were hints, and glimpses of strange scars on his belly, but she never asked him questions. She feared the ugly answers would make her care about him more than she already did.

Karen felt hope burning away inside of her, and passed her time wondering if anyone had seen her lipstick message.

Did anyone believe it? Was the message too vague? Did some janitor wash it away? Would anyone call the police? Could she really be condemned to spend the rest of her life in a trunk, the carefully tended baggage of a lunatic?

Another full moon came and went, and the legion of deep bite marks covering the back of her legs throbbed and oozed. The biting was the only thing that calmed Steven down on a full moon. He fed her horse-size penicillin pills to keep the bites from getting infected, but she was allergic to them and broke out in hives. She was itching herself by rubbing back and forth on the rough carpet of the Impala when she heard the police sirens.

She felt the Impala speed up for a moment and she thought Steven might try to outrun the cop. Then she felt the car shake as it crested onto the rough shoulder of the road to stop.

Karen heard Steven yell to her, sternly.

"Don't say a word, not one Goddamn thing. I love you and they can't have you. Don't make me prove it."

Karen heard the crunch of the officer's boots on the roadway as he approached the car, and she pressed her head against the upholstery, straining to hear whatever she could.

Her heart was thumping in her head and she could barely hear a word over her own pulse and the idle of the boat-size car.

She heard both of their voices growing loud; Steven's taking on an incredulous and angry tone. She prayed Steven wouldn't shoot the cop.

Hope rushed through her whole body and she felt like screaming, "I'm in here! I'm in the trunk!"

The officer would save her and then she'd be free!

Free.

Free to return home to her thankless job and her overwhelming debt and her resentful kids who never called. Free to re-enter the dating scene as a scarred, forty-two-year-old ex-abductee. Free to fall asleep, crying and alone, between cold sheets. Free to be avoided and scorned. Free to be unwanted, unneeded.

Free to be alone.

She found herself silent, her scream for help stillborn as a sigh.

The concept of freedom became terrible. She found herself praying for the meddling police officer to go away.

She pressed tighter against the back of the seat and heard Steven's voice.

"Yes, sir, absolutely, and thank you for pointing that out! I appreciate your concern!"

Later that night, while Steven carefully tended to Karen's bite wounds, he told her about the blown tail light on the Impala. They both laughed at their unexpected brush with the outside world.

As Karen drifted off to sleep she smelled iodine and felt it soaking into her wounds. The moon was thin outside, and her pain was at low tide. She found herself taking the strangest comfort in the fact that Steven kept her teeth in his pants pocket.

Such was love.

Laws of Virulence

INTERNAL MEMO: 08/07/2010

CASE: F-DPD0758 (CDC NORS-Water Report ID VEC147, Received 08/03/2010 via State Report OMB No. 0920-0004, Submitted by: Dr. Lorena Santos of Pacific Grace Clinic)

ETIOLOGY: Unknown (comparative specimen analysis in progress, genus/species/serotype may require new designations)

CONTAMINATION FACTOR: C-N/A, Unknown

SURVIVAL FACTOR: S-N/A, Deaths can be attributed to case though comparable pathogens have displayed symbiotic behavior

DOCUMENT INSERT: Verbatim transcript of post-containment etiology determination interview with Subject 5 (Matthew Hall). Due to active vector status (transmission mode remains classified as Indeterminate/Other/Unknown although enteric Phase 1 possible) subject interviewed in iso via 2-way audio. DPDx program active/engaged. Elimination & Control team at ready.

Recorded at Director's Request/Classified Confidential 1-A. Speaking: DPD Director Cliff Selzer, Matthew Hall

CS: Hello, Mr. Hall.

MH: [No response]

CS: I'm going to be frank with you, Mr. Hall... Can I call you Matthew?

MH: You can call me whatever you want.

CS: Very well, Matthew. I need you to understand the situation we're in right now. How important you are. How much you can help us.

MH: I'm not important. I'm the least important person you've ever met. And I don't give a shit about helping you. And if you don't get me something stiffer than this glass of fucking tap water then I'm not saying a word.

CS: Matthew, I'm afraid that water is all we can provide you right now. But if you cooperate there could be adjustments to your Stay Profile.

MH: You get me a bottle of Maker's and a shotgun. You promise that. Then I'll tell you everything.

CS: You know I can't do that.

MH: I don't know what you can or can't do. I don't even know who the hell you are. You strip me naked. You spray me down with some kind of goddamn fire extinguisher and make me sit in the dark in three smaller and smaller rooms. I thought you were cooking me alive in the last one.

CS: Matthew, that was all for standard decontamination protocol. We're trying to protect you and others.

MH: So am I safe now?

CS: "Safe?"

MH: Decontaminated?

CS: [Long pause] We're not sure, Matthew. That's why it's so important you tell us what you know.

MH: [Garbled] fucking shitbirds. Just let me die. Please.

CS: That's very selfish, Matthew. There are millions of people in this country who don't want to die, and you're putting them at risk. If you won't speak with me will you at least consider filling out the form we've placed in front of you?

MH: [Sound of pen being thrown across room, striking floor. Sound of Subject 5 expectorating on form CS115.]

BREAK IN RECORDING

MH: Now that's more like it, chief. Aaah, that's more like it.

CS: I suggest you slow down, Matthew. We don't know how alcohol will affect the specimen or its interaction with your body.

MH: [Sound of gulping.] Shit on your specimen, chief. [Sound of belch.] Oh, Jesus, that fucking burns.

CS: It's 100 proof, Matthew.

MH: No, not the booze. That stuff is silky. It's the fucking crawler. Sonofabitch never stops working on me. I knew it. Your precious little detox rooms were a waste. [Sound of fabric rubbing on skin.] See, my mouth is already bleeding. Then I'll get the fucking seaweed eyes. Then you guys will wish you already would've given me that shotgun.

CS: "Seaweed eyes?"

MH: Yeah. It's like lace under the eyes, or like... like they're bloodshot but the blood is dark green.

CS: And your wife displayed this condition?

MH: Claire had it first, and then...

CS: Then your daughter?

MH: [Long pause. Sound of gulping.] Yeah... Myra.

CS: We've performed a full sweep of your apartment, Matthew. We're aware of your loss and I promise you we understand how difficult this must be.

MH: Did you burn them?

CS: No. Our procedure dictates a course other than destruction…

MH: Quit fucking around and burn them. Please. Give them that. Claire always wanted to be cremated and… I was going to do it myself, before you guys booted in my goddamn door… please. It's the last good thing I can do for them.

CS: The sooner we know what you know, the sooner we can honor your request.

MH: Promise?

CS: We will do our best to keep funeral processing in motion.

MH: Well, cheers to that. [Sound of gulping.]

CS: So, at what point did you notice the discoloration in your wife's eyes? And were there any notable signs or symptoms prior to that? Vomiting? Fever? Abdominal cramps?

MH: There are probably some symptoms I didn't even notice. To be honest, we weren't talking that much. I mean, this all happened last week and it happened so fast. But she was always bitching and crunching on Tums and popping Tylenol, so… I mean, running a daycare center is hard work. She used to joke that children could only grow by stealing your energy and happiness. But she liked it, she really did. Hell, she was pretty much raising Myra without me.

CS: Our records indicate you lived together.

MH: [Brief laughter.] Depends on how you define living, chief. We split rent on an apartment and had the same last name, you know ...Sometimes I'd take Myra to the park. She was too little to go on the swings or anything, but she liked to smell the flowers and watch the other kids play... But Claire would have been the second person, after me of course, to tell you that I'm a piece of shit. A real charity case. So the truth is that I didn't notice how wrong things were until they'd gone way past wrong.

CS: What did you observe first?

MH: Well, I woke up after Claire every day, and I'd make the bed to pretend I was useful in some way, and I noticed some little spots of blood on her pillow. Nothing too serious looking. But then she got home that night and had a hefty cough. Plus, her breath had become pretty toxic. She'd block it with her hand but the smell would float across the whole room. And this smell, chief, it was like a dead hooker's pussy stuffed with old shrimp. But worse. It crawled into your nose like it was living. She started burning nag champa incense, so she must have smelled it too.

CS: Is that when she decided to go to the hospital?

MH: No. Claire is... Claire was a tough one. I was starting to feel a little sick, too, and Claire figured we had some food poisoning. It was her birthday a few days before, and I'd been out "job hunting" at the Pussycat Palace. You know the place?

CS: I'm aware of it.

MH: So you've seen Cherry Headrush dance before?

CS: No, Matthew. But I'm aware of many venues and chains because of their prominence on our regional disease vector maps.

MH: Oh. Shit. [Sound of gulping.] Well, I'd flipped for this girl, Cherry. And they'd just extended my unemployment for another three months so I was feeling flush. Spent almost my whole check in one afternoon, hogging up the lap dances. Milking a cheap beer buzz for hours. And then my cell started vibrating and a Reminder message pops up: CLAIRE B-DAY DINNER TONIGHT. Only the "tonight" is spelled like 2-N-I-T-E which means Claire programmed this into my phone so I'd remember. [Long pause.]

CS: Please continue. The food poisoning?

MH: So I'm running late, very buzzed and most of my cash is already in the Pussycat's sterilizer. But I have to try and pull myself out of this so I hit Chinatown and looked for something fancy to cook up. Chan's Market has a beautiful red snapper on discount, so I cop that, pick up some lemon and capers, and get two fancy chocolate Cupcakes at Dreampuff's.

SEE SEPARATE DOCUMENT INSERT FOR RELATED DIRECTOR ORDER: DPDx multi-venue deploy/search/surveil. Full containment authorized. Andolini appointed Team Leader.

CS: Sorry about that break, Matthew. You've been very helpful.

MH: Do I have any choice? Really? I appreciate the second bottle, but you might want to give me a bucket if I'm going to keep going. Although I'd have no problem shellacking your little desk here.

CS: Consider us well-advised. Please continue.

MH: Shit, man… it seems obvious, doesn't it? I barely had any time to bake the fish before Claire got home with Myra. I brushed up and changed my clothes and put on some Alicia Keys even though I can't stand that shit. Lit a couple of tea lights I found under the sink. But I still fucked it up. I still fucked it up. [Pause] The fish looked good by candle-light. Looked delicious.

CS: You think the red snapper was the original source of the sickness?

MH: Thing is, I was pulling off the sober act, but I had to burp. And that just ruined it. One hundred percent. Like a strip club came out of my mouth. Claire pegged it, and laid into me, even though Myra was sitting in the room in her little bouncy chair and we'd sworn not to fight in front of her. And I mentioned that and we tried to enjoy the dinner and pretend that something was okay and nice and we didn't even notice how raw the snapper was until we'd taken out half of the fish.

CS: So Claire was guessing that the raw fish had given each of you food poisoning?

MH: Yeah. She was toughing it out until Myra got sick, too. Because that didn't make any sense. Myra was still breast-feeding, so she never had any of that nasty snapper. But she was coughing and having the blood speckles just the same.

CS: That's when she visited Pacific Grace, toward the beginning of August?

MH: I think so. I was sort of on my own thing while this was happening. Sleeping on the couch at night. Hiding at Pussycat's during the day. I told myself I was in exile, giving Claire some space to forgive me. But I was really just doing the same old shit. Living in a worn down strip club booth, paying Cherry to hip-hump me. Hoping that Claire and Myra would start feeling better. That maybe Claire would start feeling so good she'd build up the mojo to finally drop me.

CS: When did you find out she wasn't feeling better?

MH: Well, Pussycat's kind of extradited me back to my family. I was already putting off that rotten jellyfish smell and… let's just say there aren't enough dollars to make a stripper let you cough blood in her face. I didn't even see it coming. Just sitting there half-chubbed and dead drunk and BOOM! No tickle in the throat. No warning.

CS: Do you happen to know Cherry Headrush's real name?

MH: You're kidding, right? [Sound of bottle opening/sound of gulping.] All I know is that I was home and starting to feel pretty rotten myself, and I can't imagine how Claire was managing to run the daycare like that. All those little people screaming. "I want. I need. Watch me. Love me." Jesus.

CS: This was the Morning Sun Daycare on Stanton?

MH: Yup. So, Claire stumbles into the house and she and Myra are both coughing and they have those triple-dark circles under their eyes, and seeing them like that makes me feel like I managed to sneak into Hell without dying. Just worthless. No, worse than that—fucking evil. [Long pause] Claire said the lady at the hospital gave them both two I.V. bags to rehydrate them, and that they needed to go back tomorrow for more diagnostics. But she thought it might be a parasite, like one of those squiggly little gut worms you get from eating sushi in Ohio.

CS: Did she suggest you go with them?

MH: Of course. And I was thinking it was the right thing to do. I was starting to feel weak in my bones. But the next morning I wake up and they're already gone and there's a text on my phone saying that they're both "feeling much better." Which was weird, because they'd been coughing like crazy all night. Just brutal sounding. Wet. Like I'd guess TB used to sound.

CS: So... a productive cough followed by an apparent return to vigor?

MH: Sure, chief. However you want to call it. It spooked me

because I was still under the weather. But I pegged that up in my mind as booze-related immune suppression. All those sauced little white blood cells getting bitch-slapped by the bugs in my system.

SEE SEPARATE DOCUMENT INSERT RE: Viability of ethanol [or variant] ingestion as chemical deterrent to life cycle of [un-named parasite/parasitoid CASE: F-DPD0758].

CS: So when did it become evident that Claire and Myra were still... unwell?

MH: [Prolonged sound of gulping.] You want to hear the rest, you get me a loaded shotgun. I promise I'll only fire it once.

CS: Not an option, Matthew.

MH: Okay. Fuck it. I better get the truth out before the goddamn crawler starts telling my story. [Pause/sound of shuddering exhalation.] I knew they were still unwell when I found their tongues. Claire's was in the bed, tucked under a pillow. Dried up already, like jerky. And Myra's...

CS: Please, Matthew.

MH: Myra's was in her crib, next to her favorite pacifier, the one with the orange dolphin on the back. And I've got to tell you, chief, between my half-sick, half-drunk stupor and lack of sleep, I felt like I was dreaming. So I did what seemed like the right thing. I threw the tongues in the garbage and kept on tidying the apartment. Like I could organize away what I was seeing. Like I could clean up reality.

SEE SEPARATE DOCUMENT INSERT FOR RELATED DIRECTOR ORDER: DPDx forensic detachment to attain SW Sanitation schedule/potential combing of landfill [use of trailing dogs authorized]. Retention of tissue from Subjects 3 and 4 Top Priority, presence/absence of eggs to be communicated ASAP.

MH (continued): So I had the place pretty spruced, and I was waiting for them to come home. Claire wasn't answering her phone. And my nerves were on four alarm blaze, so I had some bourbon close by, just to keep things mellow until I could figure out what was going on. I'd call her phone. Five rings. Voice mail. Nothing. Take a swig. Five rings. Voice mail. Nothing. And they still weren't home by 9:00pm.

CS: Records show you called Claire's mother.

MH: Three or four times. But she never picked up. And I thought about calling the cops, but I knew my speech was slurring by that point. What would I tell them? There was no crime, and they'd probably guess it was just another wife bailing with the kid, leaving the stew-bum behind.

CS: But their tongues? That must have…

MH: Can't see that impressing the cops either. Just a way to induce them to pack a straitjacket. Besides, if I mentioned finding their tongues… I'd been on a steady drunk trying to bury that detail, hoping I was just losing my shit.

CS: So when did you next see Claire and Myra?

MH: Never again. I think the night they came home from the doctor's was the last time I really saw them.

CS: Matthew, the chronology we've established shows the three of you were in that apartment for almost two days before we…

MH: Before you decided to bust into my place and stop me from finishing my work? Listen, chief, this is hard enough to talk about. So let me lay it out for you without all of your interjections and then we can clear up your questions later.

CS: [Long pause.]

MH: That's more like it. So what I'm saying is that I saw Claire and Myra again, but they sure as shit weren't my Claire and Myra. At some point that night I'd finished my bottle and given up on my phone crusade. I remember thinking, "She finally left me." And I remember feeling so relieved. No one would expect anything from me after that, you know? I'd cop some menial job, enough to service a studio apartment and child support. I'd push for a few weekends a month with Myra, just enough to not feel guilty when I show some stripper a picture of my kid. I think I'd been waiting for a long time for a chance to fall apart.

CS: Matthew, I need to know more about your wife and child, and time is a factor. We have a staff psychologist you can speak with later if you need to get more familial issues off your chest.

MH: Courtesy is a short-lived thing around here, huh, chief? All right then, shitbird... So I passed out on the couch, if you can believe it. Noble. Noble guy. And when I woke up they were sitting at the foot of the couch, both of them, very quietly and... holy shit... and Claire was nursing Myra, and her head was tilted, and she was staring across the room at nothing, like she was back on Paxil, and they both had those goddamn seaweed eyes. And Claire had both of her breasts out and the one that wasn't in Myra's mouth was... it was kind of lumpy, like it had been stuffed with tapioca, and the nipple looked raw, just red meat raw, with these blisters around it, some popped, some filled up with the same dark green that was in her eyes, and...

CS: Hold on for a moment please, Matthew.

SEE SEPARATE DOCUMENT INSERT RE: Confirmation of multiple gender-specific intra-species transmission methods as seen in CASE: F-DPD0674. Student population under Sector 6 Quarantine should immediately be grouped same sex for confirmation/testing of all fluids for presence of concurrent microparasites.

CS: Okay, we're back, Matthew.

MH: [Garbled/indistinct vulgarity.] My tongue is starting to feel numb. [Sound of coughing/spitting]. Aw, Christ, chief.

CS: I'd suggest drinking some water. We need you to finish your account.

MH: Yeah, well... suggest in one hand and spit in the other and see which one fills up first. [Sound of laughter/sound of gulping/sound of empty bottle set down on table.] What you have to understand is that I thought I was dreaming, seeing Claire and Myra like that. Between the guilt and the hooch, that kind of nightmare fits right in. But then Claire put one of her bony bird hands on my ankle and she turned toward me and smiled. And I swear to God, these two wiry antennae uncurled from in between her teeth and started swaying in the air. So of course I lost my shit. I rolled onto my side and chucked out my guts on the shag carpet, and it's just bile and bourbon and I get that post-puke rush where things feel okay for a moment and I'm thinking I'm awake now and then I turn back towards Claire. [Long pause] She's still smiling at me and this voice comes out of her mouth and says, "Empty. Feed." And she's got her other breast cupped and I swear it's dribbling this shit like fucking wheat grass juice. [Pause] And Myra... Myra pulls off the other breast, or at least her lips move away, but there's something else pushing out of her mouth, something with those same feelers wiggling, and it's latched on to Claire, right on her tit, and it's got these two tiny claws pinched on and its body is pulsing and hunching, and these plates on its back are clicking together and I can see through this thing's belly, where the skin is clear and its guts are filling up green. And Myra's eyes look almost black, but I can still tell they're rolling back in her head...

CS: Claire could speak?

MH: They both could. But Myra... she didn't have any words yet, so she would smile and her lips would pull back, but all that came out... Have you ever seen that footage of dolphins being massacred in Japan? And Claire's voice was different. There was a lisp, like her mouth was too full, and there was a sort of hissing to it, like cricket legs or... [Pause] And the smell that came from them filled up the room. It was like being stuck in the dumpster behind a seafood wholesaler on a hundred degree day. Made me throw up again.

CS: So why didn't you call 911?

MH: Are you listening to me, chief? This strikes you as a rational response fucking situation? I had no bearings. I asked Claire a question, thinking that this time she'd give me a normal answer in her old, sweet voice and I'd be all the way awake, but it came out with no authority and just made me feel smaller and detached and more alone. But I told her I was worried and that I wondered where she was yesterday and she smiled again... I'm thinking that's the only way the thing could move around in there... and all she says is, "Work. Feeding." And I say, "You were at the daycare?" She nods and says, "Feeding. Growing. Most will be born." Then she looks down at Myra, and her nose curls up like she's disgusted, and she says, "This one is dying. This one is too small." [Long pause/sound of soft crying.]

CS: Matthew, I'm sorry. I'm so sorry. But the more detail...

MH: Details, chief? Go fuck yourself. I did what I did. I tried to save them. I tried to fix it. To fix them before anybody would have to know… But it was too late. I could barely stand, but Claire was always pretty frail, and this fucking bug thing had wiped her out. So I tried to help her first and it wasn't too difficult to get her hands belted behind her, but that thing… that thing had teeth or mandibles or whatever and Claire started to shake and even with all the lamps in the room turned on my head kept making a shadow over her face and Myra was squealing and stomping her heels down where I left her on the carpet and I couldn't tell where the thing in Claire's mouth ended and the rest of her tongue began and when I cut in with the box knife it started bleeding so bad… But for just a moment Claire was looking straight at me, and even with the green lace it looked like her old eyes and then she spit right in my face. Right in my face, and she meant it. And her mouth was half-filled, and I noticed the blood from the thing and my wife wouldn't quite mix, so there's your details chief. Then her lips pulled back and the eyes were still Claire's eyes and she said, "You did this to us."

CS: Matthew, she…

MH: She was right. She was right. Even after I managed to finish cutting through, and I'd pulled the goddamn thing out of her face and smashed it under my foot… You want more details? The shell of the thing started changing colors and it hissed and sprayed a yellow mist out of its mouth after I set it on the floor. What the fuck does that? Even after I got the thing out of Claire she still had her eyes trained on me, just bullet-eyes, and she couldn't have hated me any more. And I couldn't fix her, because she was already weak and I don't think she could stop from choking on all that blood.

But I thought that Myra... [Long pause.]

CS: You didn't try to remove the "crawler?"

MH: I didn't want her to bleed like Claire. So I thought if I could just kill the bug that maybe it would just detach and... and I was thinking of how they cook lobsters, and I tried to keep the water in a tin can and hold her over it, but the steam was making everything slick and I couldn't get her mouth open at the same time and... so I thought that the burns would heal, you know how they say that the inside of your mouth can heal so fast, and then at least she'd live, and I didn't put the sponge in there for more than twenty seconds, but the thing was hissing and it tried to curl in on itself, and Myra started shaking and making fists and then her eyes were open and they were looking right at me, right into me, and...

CS: Matthew?

MH: They were right. There's nothing... [Sound of empty glass bottle being shattered.]

CS: Matthew, please. There's no need to...

MH: I did this. I did this. I... [Sound of Subject 5 collapsing on floor. Sound of wet coughs/exhalations. Faint sound of specimen clicking/squealing from interior of Subject 5. Sound of door opening/boots shuffling/Subject 5 moved to stretcher.]

CS: Goddamn it, [REDACTED]. I said plastic bottles only. Triage?

DPDx: Subject 5 at ISS 75. Both major sources of blood flow to brain severed, trachea punctured. He was committed.

CS: The specimen?

DPDx: Significant damage. Suggest immediate retrieval attempt.

CS: Agreed. Prepare for transfer to Surgical Theater 8, movement protocol in place.

DPDx: Confirmed. [Brief pause.] Director?

CS: Yes?

DPDx: If I didn't know better, I'd think this dead fuck was grinning right at me.

CS: Could be a symptom of the parasite attempting to exit the damaged host. Stay far from his mouth until we've assessed specimen mobility. And let's keep it moving. Perhaps Matthew's got a second chance at fatherhood.

DPDx: [Muffled laughter] Yes, sir. Rolling out.

END TRANSCRIPT

The Brilliant Idea

You had the brilliant idea this morning, at dawn.

You rose to a noise from outside, a trashcan overturned by wind, spilling fetid food for early-rising dogs. In this moment—sleep a mucous haze over your dilated eyes, mouth tasting soured bacteria, hearing the clang of metal against concrete—the idea landed.

It was genius, the answer to every question you'd ever given up answering, the unifying concept that could surely explain God to the world in a way that we could all agree on.

This idea was too big. Maybe it's the sheer processing speed required. Synaptic overload. That Ambien you took. Your brain couldn't hold it. The further your eyes opened, the more this idea slipped away like the organs of a suddenly skinned man.

Then you were Awake—not in some grand spiritual sense, but the corporal—and the brilliant idea was gone.

All that remains is this phantom feeling that you *knew*... something.

Tears come. They are extra-salty; you drank too much wine last night.

Skipping your morning habits, you shelve your shower and your half-conscious masturbation and instead sit at the kitchen table with a pad of paper, scrawling words like "stardust" and "sub-cellular." But they're never more than words.

You head outside; start knocking over trashcans. Perhaps there's an auditory trigger? Each can produces a clang before fast-food bags tumble free and grease their way into the gutter.

Nothing.

The world needs this idea.

You drink, smoke, meditate.

You create Goldbergian devices—alarm clock/sewing machines that drive needles into the soft pads of your feet, causing you to wake suddenly.

Months pass. You can't focus. Your job's terminated.

Despondent, walking home, you barely notice the semi-truck running a red as you shuffle through the crosswalk.

The horn sounds. Headlights fill your vision.

The brilliant idea is there, glowing, closer, closer, almost within your grasp.

Then it hits you.

Branded

The fucking mark. Raised, ropy-white and red-rimmed. A thick, knotty scar. Had it been a simple straight line, like an incision scar, I certainly could have moved beyond my revulsion. Love would have overcome and all that. Of course, this wasn't any simple incision scar. It was a fully 3-D scar that looked worse than the initial wound, and it was in the *exact* shape of the McDonald's logo. Goddamned Golden Arches. Only the scar was more sickly white than golden, and clear of any of the tiny, downy blonde hairs that rested near it. Upon first finding the scar, which was just to the inside of her right thigh, I laughed. AHA, so she tried to play a joke on me. A real josher, using prosthetic scars to gross me out. Ha-ha, very funny, now *TAKE IT OFF!*

One look in her eyes and I see that the scar is real, and there's no way in hell she wants to tell me about how she got it. Now she looks worried, like this is when guys always bail out. I can't leave her, as much as my guts churn and threaten to spill out of my mouth. Plus, I'm stuck in a weird spot. To initiate a sort of deepening of our sexual relationship I had promised to go down on her. I mean, that's how I found the scar in the first place, when I was taking her shorts off. So there I was, nauseous and obligated to cunnilingus because I didn't want to be the millionth asshole guy in her life.

I closed my eyes as I began, trying to erase the image of the Golden Arches scar. As my tongue separated labia and found the clit I suddenly saw Ronald McDonald behind my closed eyelids. As my tongue urged her on my brain was awash in all things McDonald's. Grimace and the Hamburglar, sizzling greasy beef being flipped with a scummy spatula by a pimple face kid whose acne leaked yellow-red onto the skillet, smoking trails coming off the beef and pus mixture, the killing floor for McDonald's Inc, where the blood and shit rushed from millions of Heifers as they mooed their last terrified moo, a boy covered in burn scars asking me if I wanted fries with that, chickens shitting into six slightly similar McNugget molds, lick lick back and forth surging in to suppress my scar-induced nausea.

The more my tongue pressed the pink the more she tasted like fancy ketchup. When she came she tightened her thighs and the scar pressed deep into my left cheek. For a moment I was marked too. I flinched. She noticed.

She was a wonderful human being, with a laugh that you'd want to hear at the gates of heaven.

And I am weak for leaving her.

Sparklers Burning

Martin set down the shoebox full of fingers that he was carrying to the kitchen and picked up the remote. He thought, "I've been working hard today. Why not relax for a moment and see who's talking on my box?"

The T.V. sparked on with a static crackle, shedding vivid light into the previously jet black room. Martin couldn't believe his luck. He thought, "I didn't even have to flip no channels and there you are. Yes, yes, yes. There you are."

The perfectly bland face of Sunny Potterton smiled its chipper and highly marketable smile right at Martin. Sunny's teeth were so bright they seemed to glow between her thin, red lips. Her bob-cut, blonde hair hung silky aside from the straight-placed part down the center. Sunny was saying something about the alkaline levels in a good garden, and Martin was listening intently.

"Oh, God I love you, Sunny!" Martin said it aloud in his living room, loving the way her name felt as he manifested it with breath. "Sunny, Sunny, Sunny!"

Martin did love her, and to prove it to Sunny he watched her whenever she was on the talking box, and he bought all of her magazines, the home craft ones, and the wedding ones, and even the baby ones, in spite of the fact that babies gave him the willies to hell and back. Martin even bought some of the Sunny Potterton stock the day it hit the market, and he didn't get mad when it tanked just days later.

Sunny was clean, polite, well spoken, and almost universally loved. Martin realized that he was none of these things, but he was willing to improve, and he worked hard to make his life something special.

He stood in his living room, slack-jawed, wearing a pair of blood-stained tan boxer shorts, watching Sunny Potterton plant tulips.

Martin's left eyelid began to twitch and pulse with his heartbeat, causing him to grimace. The room was quickly filling up with the chemical smell of hot metal, and Martin recoiled, taking a step back from the T.V. The talking box was starting to glow, giving Martin an instant and pounding pain in his chest. Martin thought that it might be sending out some kind of signal that would erase his heart.

The unpleasant thought passed when he heard Sunny's voice speaking to him from the television.

"Martin, do you mind if I come in?"

The thought of having Sunny Potterton over for a visit overwhelmed Martin and he felt faint, but managed to nod Yes.

The talking box began to glow even brighter, and Martin watched it give birth to Sunny Potterton. The image of the garden on the television was rendered down the middle, cleaved in half, and out of the dark static oval at the center a hand emerged, shiny with fluid. The hand was delicate and had beautiful purple finger nails. It was followed by a shoulder and a head, pushing out with great exertion, and then there was an explosive belching sound followed by a wet thud as Sunny was birthed into Martin's living room, soaking wet on his old shag carpet.

Sunny began to dry immediately, sloughing off the shiny sac that she arrived in. She vomited up a puddle of what appeared to be television static and turned to Martin.

"So good of you to have me to your house!" she said with a voice that Martin knew must be full of Christmas cheer all year round.

"So, Martin, what have you been up to?"

"Well…Sunny…"

He couldn't believe this was happening, and reached his right hand out to touch Sunny. His finger was greeted by a strong electric shock that relayed itself to his brain and extremities and nearly floored him.

"Sorry, Martin, I'm still an electronic transmission."

Martin frowned, realizing he couldn't get as close to Sunny as he wanted to without taking a nasty jolt. He wondered if an electronic transmission could bleed.

"No, I won't bleed, Martin. I can tell what you're thinking and I don't have to tell you I frown on discourtesy."

"Sorry, Sunny. Why have you come to visit me?"

"Well, Martin, I've come to help you with your spring cleaning."

Martin wondered at Sunny's perfect timing. He'd already been cleaning for days, and now he had the world's foremost cleaning expert in his own house as a special helper.

Martin thought that God must finally be rewarding him for all the hard work he'd done on his Sparkle Shrine. This electronic Sunny was his prize for years of working in the shadows, carving skin and bone and muscle, killing only those who would not be missed. The Sparkle Shrine was not yet completed, so Martin was surprised that God had responded so prematurely. Maybe this was a test…

"Okay, Sunny, you can help me with my spring cleaning, and then I'll show you what you were sent here to see."

Sunny smiled, sunshine bleach bright teeth gleaming.

"Okay, Martin, let's get to work."

Martin and digital Sunny scoured the house, soaking floors in bleach, spreading potpourri, and opening windows to let in the cool night air. Martin did most of the manual labor while Sunny gave instructions and offered advice.

"You can get rid of all that hair in the dishwasher by adding a saline solution next time you run a hot cycle."

And

"A heavy cologne, one with a real musk to it, will not only cover up the smell of the cordite but mask any traces."

And

"You know a simple flower trim would really make that vat of acid more of a centerpiece and bring a sense of light to your basement."

And

"If you shift these body parts to Tupperware and refrigerate them they'll last much longer than in your standard shoebox."

Martin was glowing, bright with his own sweat and reflecting the static shimmer of Sunny Potterton's electric skin.

After six steady hours of intensive cleaning Martin was wiped out, aching at every joint. Sunny urged him toward further work but he was fatigued beyond his limits, and believed he had proven himself. He was ready to show Sunny the Sparkle Shrine.

At his request, Sunny followed Martin up to his bedroom. Her feet singed the carpet beneath her, trailing tiny wisps of smoke.

Once upstairs, Martin led Sunny to his bedroom. He opened the door for her and walked past the large man who was tied to his bed. The man was bald, naked, soaked to the bone with sweat, and bleeding from the inside of his left eye where Martin had previously performed a home lobotomy. He was bound to the bed with piano wire sunk deep into his wrists and ankles, and his mouth was gagged with duct tape and an oven mitt. Part of the man's small intestine had been pulled through an incision in the skin of his belly, and hung wet to his left side.

The man was surrounded by arts and crafts supplies, poster boards, twine, glue sticks, stamps, pinking shears, and shiny star stickers, the same kind that Sunny used on her show. The man woke as Sunny and Martin entered the room, and passed back into unconsciousness seconds later, his eyes rolling, showing their whites.

Martin paid no attention to the man. He knelt before Sunny and asked if she wanted to see his Shrine. She sighed and said, "Yes."

Martin looked to the sky, whispered, "Please let her love it," and opened the door to the converted closet.

The black pixels at the center of Sunny's electronic eyes multiplied as her pupils dilated. She was the first witness to Martin's life's work.

Flesh was tanned and strapped around bones, bones were bound by tendons, tendons crisscrossed and were nailed into the wall with pushpins. Bowls sat in a perfect circle around the mass of tissue, each bowl containing a preserved body part. There were shriveled eyes, lips, noses, testicles, labia, fingers, ears, nipples, tongues.

Martin's favorite part of the whole thing was the glitter. He had covered everything in glitter, gold and purple and green glitter, so that it sparkled in even the faintest light.

He felt his face flush with blood and pride as he turned to Sunny for approval.

Martin felt the world turn to liquid beneath his feet when he saw Sunny frowning.

Martin felt the world turn to shame as Sunny's face changed and twisted, darkened. Sunny's bronzed skin and high cheekbones had become sullen and scrunched.

"Well, Martin, I can appreciate your work ethic here. You've certainly been laboring away, and I appreciate the symmetry, but..."

Martin's heart kept sinking, deeper and deeper still.

"...but, frankly, it's sub-par work. The glitter seems, well, amateurish, and the arrangement of bits and pieces is ultimately distracting. It takes away from whatever meager power the main attraction may have had. Also, and I hope you've picked up on this too, it reeks of death. Bleach is a must, my friend."

"But, Sunny..."

"Please don't interrupt me, Martin. I've enjoyed our time together, and I hope you have too, but I've got to be going. Just one final bit of cleaning to be done..."

The look in Sunny's eyes changed. Her brow furrowed and shadows filled her eye sockets.

"Martin, do you know what an aberration is?"

"Nope, Sunny. Why? Do I have one? If I show you my aberration will you stay here?"

"No, Martin. An aberration is something that must be cleansed from every surface. It is something so dirty that the world can't tolerate it."

Sunny took another carpet-singe step towards Martin.

"The weird thing about aberrations is that they're supposed to be self-destructive, but every once in a while they mutate and survive. It's very…un-tidy. So, someone else must clean them up. I'm a professional, trust me on this."

She reached out and touched Martin's chest. His heart seized up and rattled his ribcage with tight tremors. He collapsed to the floor, sending shock-spirals of glitter into the air. He couldn't move. He struggled for breath and watched Sunny clean his bedroom.

He watched, weak and helpless, as Sunny Potterton gingerly disassembled his life's work. He watched her static soaked hands systematically shatter the carefully bound bones of his Sparkle Shrine.

He watched as Sunny delicately opened the mouth of the man in his bed. She pried his jaw wide with one hand and then inserted the index finger of her right hand deep into his mouth, as if to pluck out a pimento that had lodged in his trachea. The man began to blister immediately as the electricity brought him a quick death.

Martin's chest tightened again, and he had to gulp down breath between pounding heartbeats. He hung his head and struggled to breathe as the electric Sunny destroyed all he had created.

He was shocked to find he could feel everything she was doing in *his* hands and body.

In the aftermath of the attack the air was thick with the cloying smell of exposed rot. Martin was curled into fetal position on the floor. He could no longer see Sunny and wondered where she had gone.

He heard a voice, familiar and somehow still comforting, calling to him.

"Martin…Martin…"

It was Sunny. She was calling to him from his living room.

He stood and stumbled toward her. He followed her burning footsteps in the carpet down the stairs and into the living room, where he saw her crouched in front of the television, one hand already immersed in its glowing surface.

"I've got to go back, Martin. I've got a rigorous schedule, and I feel my work is done here. Overall I love what you've done with the place. Maybe I'll see you again."

The black oval in the center of Martin's talking box opened wide and pulled Sunny back in, sealing off with the sound of Sunny's cold, business-like laughter.

Martin reached out to the glowing screen where Sunny was talking about the seasonal life of orchids. He wanted so badly to be in there with her, especially now that his life here had been destroyed. He watched her soft, blonde hair lilting in the autumn wind; saw her hands diving into black soil to make room for seeds. He wanted to be with her. He thought that he might be able to make Sunny bleed in that world, if he could get in. He grabbed the sides of the talking box, reared his head back, and swung it forward.

A corona of fire bloomed from the glass where his head shattered the screen. Electricity sparkled across the surface of his blackened flesh like so much glitter.

Simple Equations

Minna knew that her fits were a blessing. She'd never stated this fact to anyone. Not her husband Jakob, nor her son Garin. Not even to her mother, who Minna knew viewed the writhing black-outs as a curse which might one day steal away her precious child.

At the funeral Minna had wondered if her mother might still be alive, had she understood the nature of the attacks. Perhaps the heart-crushing stress of caring for a tormented child would have been alleviated if Minna could have explained the glorious *glow* that she felt during the fits.

Her mother could only have seen the child, and later the young woman, in a state of extreme duress. Eyes rolled white. Teeth gnashing. Back arched in a contorted "U" that threatened to snap the spine and spread open her stretched-thin belly. She could never have known the sights, the glow, that Minna had experienced as her body bore its own assault.

Inside that state Minna had seen new worlds. Alien languages formed by numbers and angles and whorls, and images of a galaxy in which forces shifted gloriously. Minna had seen these images from so great a distance that all the chaos and movement had been reduced to simple truths, which she later learned to speak about and document to great effect at the Technical University in Darmstadt.

As a child she called these things she'd witnessed The Beauties. As a woman she relented and referred to them under the name which her male counter-parts at University used: Physics.

But in her heart, still: The Beauties.

And the things she witnessed during her fits served her well, or as well as they could. Her brilliance with the language of movement allowed her occasion to matriculate and complete a doctorate at Technical. Although she was forbidden from filling an academic post, the sheer value of her knowledge permitted her to work—always unofficially—alongside minds like Hemholtz and Muller. She aided Wuerzberg with his radar research at Telefunken.

She was afforded little to no wage for these efforts, but found the opportunity to test the ideas of Prandtl, or dissect the effects of flow velocity, too alluring.

It was her chance, in each of these studies, to speak the language of The Beauties outside of the blinding moments in which she'd envisioned them. It felt heretical to do anything else.

And now her talent with "physics" had brought her to Nordhausen in the Harz Mountains, as the primary member of an airborne weapons development group.

It was here that she'd had her most recent and terrible fit. Terrible because during her last attack the glow had abandoned her.

She'd seen nothing, knew nothing of the fit until it was over. And instead of coming to with an even more keen sense of how the world was, indeed, in exact order, she woke to the realization that something inside of her had broken.

She'd pleaded for her husband Jakob then, called out for him to lift her from the floor of her small house. Such was her agitation upon recovery—she had forgotten Jakob had perished three years before in France, when the war had not yet seemed real to her. She'd called out for her son Garin, too, who had been away working as a guard at the Maidanek camp for as long as Jakob had been dead and buried.

Minna was finally found there on the floor, soaked through from exertion, by a Nordhausen guard on night duty.

She'd asked to be shipped out of the mountains, to see a doctor better than Kuntzler, who she knew was fiercely held in the grip of alcohol at most hours, but due to "security reasons" she was never allowed to leave the factory grounds.

She knew too much about the weapons program to risk transporting. Kuntzler assigned her to two days of bed rest and left it at that.

Since the day of that empty, thieving fit she had been unable to move her left arm, and the left side of her face was nearly dead to the touch, its eyelid drooping so heavily it obscured and twisted her depth perception.

Worse, her thoughts and memories seemed to have been scattered to the periphery of her mind, and recalling the way to mouth a certain phrase or spell common words became a chore.

The men around her—the guards and fellow researchers and craftsmen of the Nordhausen munitions factory—now looked at her differently. She heard whispers and caught smirking glances.

As a woman she'd felt that her power at Nordhausen had always been in question; this new and damnable disability was sapping what little influence she'd once wielded.

The factory labor—hollow-faced Jews shipped over by Koch from Buchenwald—still regarded her with fear, and she cursed herself for finding comfort in that. After all, their fear was misplaced. She'd never harmed one of them. In fact, she'd quietly protested the banning of the Jews from the University back in'38, at risk to her own life. The unearthing of this fact had almost prevented her from receiving her development position at Nordhausen, but in the end the intellectual prowess and value of Minna Konig's mind had proven too valuable to the Führer's project.

Now Minna wondered how much more time she'd be allowed to complete her work. She'd been sequestered to the harsh terrain of the Harz Mountains for years now, toiling at Nordhausen to develop an un-manned flight craft that could accurately deliver bombs to the territory of their enemies.

The factory itself, aside from its attendant development offices, was a rough place. Parts of the weapon production and storage area were being built into the mountains themselves, and the laborers that toiled at this task were dying at a rate Minna found surreal. These dead men were carried out on carts, and were quickly replaced by new skeleton-thin workers.

About two months back a laborer had attempted to sabotage the massive steel press, one of the few machines too large to fit into the mountain-side tunnels. The normal punishment for this, for anything outside Nordhausen's rule of law, would be to hang the man in the gallows beside the factory. These hangings took place daily, sometimes for what seemed like hours. But the soldier in charge of the man must have grown bored with the noose.

Minna heard the story later, how the saboteur had been forced at gunpoint to wedge the upper half of his body into the press. How after the machine had done its work the other men who attended to it were forced to scrape the remains away and return to work, sliding steel plates into the maw of the blood-slicked machine.

Minna avoided these parts of the factory as often as she could. Instead she stayed in the research office, toiling away for hours with her pad and pen. It was hard work for Minna but initially she'd reveled in the language of it. Angle of attack, curvature, mass, all of it rolling like honey on her tongue as she formulated trajectories and wingspans and frame designs. Even when Jakob had passed, she refused to acknowledge the reality of what she was creating.

The ends are not important, she told herself. *The universe will work in exact order, as it always has.*

She knew she was being seduced by a chance to speak The Beauties, and to do so with greater authority than she had been able to at University. But this was knowledge that she held in utmost restraint and it only crept into her mind on long nights when she could not find sleep. It was then, as the cold winds of the Harz Mountains howled against the small frame of her house, that she allowed her mind to be over-run with thoughts of Jakob, and the terrible way the men at Nordhausen treated their labor, and the effect that her love affair with her visions might one day have on the flesh of the unsuspecting.

She could only clear these terrible thoughts by whispering the name of her son.

Garin.

Garin, please come home.

They said that a miracle had saved Garin during the American's attack on Maidanek. A bullet had glanced from his high cheekbone and proceeded to tear off a substantial portion of the left side of his skull. Somehow a field doctor had managed to escape with Garin's unconscious body and had sealed shut the wound, suturing the flap of skin and hair that had been torn loose by the gunfire.

The piece of skull lost in the injury had never been recovered, but Garin still survived the trauma. He fought a fever that peaked at one hundred and five degrees, and his body staved off an infection that threatened to creep right up to the vulnerable soft concavity where Garin's skull used to be.

Once he regained consciousness he managed to speak his mother's name. Minna was well known among the higher ranking officers, who wanted to respect Garin's apparent request.

Looking at him now, slumped forward in his wheelchair with a thin string of drool running from the right corner of his mouth to his shoulder, Minna guessed that they just wanted to be rid of him. And deep down she loathed herself for feeling the same way.

He's finally here, but he's never coming home.

It wasn't supposed to be like this. You were supposed to be here to help me.

She looked at her dead arm, saw how loose and separate it was from what she felt was her body.

I need you now. You can't need me.

She hated herself for thinking it.

Minna wondered if he was in there somewhere, thinking and struggling to speak just as she had done ever since her last fit. She hoped his mind might be healing, growing stronger.

Her eyelid was drooping less than it used to. Perhaps he was on the same slow road to recovery. In her brighter moments she believed that this was the truth and it allowed her to find her own words more easily. She'd discuss her job with him, she'd reminisce about Jakob. She even, for the first time in her life, tried to explain her vision of The Beauties to him, but gave up when her tongue couldn't find a way around the ideas.

She settled for gently washing Garin's wounds and combing his hair on the side opposite the injury. She'd tried to bathe him the week before but with one arm it had been too difficult to shift his body. On top of that, she'd noticed he'd become aroused when she'd tried to wash his groin. While Minna hadn't been disturbed by it, Garin had emitted a low moan and started to cry. As best he could, he'd tried to shake his head from left to right.

No, Mom. No.

She respected his wishes but worried that her inability to completely clean him would let infection creep back in.

Her work at Nordhausen had slowed to a near standstill. She felt a strange relief at the fact—*This weapon won't help anyone. It won't help Garin.*—but knew how dangerous it was to be of no use to the men of Nordhausen and the Reich.

How long will it be until they bring in someone like Reinholtz to continue my work?

And the jokes at her expense were beginning to feel more like threats. She heard comments about the "worthlessness of the feeble-minded," the curse of the "useless eaters" and "life unworthy of life."

Minna tried to return to her work full force, although she could get none of the men at Nordhausen, not even Kuntzler, to help attend to Garin. He was a reminder that none of them could tolerate. But Minna knew that her weapons work was the only way to return to the status quo.

If I can get this craft to fly, if we can get a few dry runs to clear the right distance, then they'll know I should remain here. Perhaps they'll even increase my wage and I can bring in an outside doctor to help Garin heal.

She worked for two days straight, coming home only to feed Garin soup—chicken noodle was his favorite but she had to make do with a thin tomato puree—and to make sure he knew he wasn't alone.

Minna prayed for another fit, something to strike her down so she could rise again and know exactly how to make the Nordhausen project a success. She focused on finding the right words and calculations until sweat dripped from her wrinkled forehead.

Her renewed efforts were working.

She designed a new wing flap that would allow the craft to stabilize even over sharp mountain winds. She perfected her fuel equation to maximize distance. She recalled bits of her work with Wuerzberg and proposed ways to equip the weapon with radar guidance.

The effort exhausted her. She requested a soldier to shuttle her home from the factory.

Her driver didn't make eye contact. He didn't speak a word.

This is wrong.

She'd had the thought so many times before—when she'd stolen from her mother to buy hard candy, when she'd tossed a book which Goebbels had banned into the pyre at University, when she'd buried Jakob, when she'd thought about all of the destruction her project might create.

But none of those moments had felt as wholly wrong as when she'd read the letter that had been delivered to her residence.

Minna had hoped that the letter might tell her that a doctor had finally been assigned to come help Garin, as she'd been requesting. Instead she'd received notice that both she and Garin were going to receive "the finest care" at the Reich Work Group of Sanatoriums and Nursing Homes.

As a scientist she was supposed to be insulated from the daily goings on of the war. But she'd heard of the Reich Work Group, and understood the nature of their "healing." Even if she could convince someone that she and Garin were becoming healthier, she was sure her University protest from '38 would resurface. She'd be shunned—they might even declare her insane for once having favored Jews.

The Reich had clearly decided, with the utter finality the Work Group represented, that Minna and Garin no longer represented the best interests of the great race.

We must escape.

As soon as she had the ridiculous thought and her mind tried to put together all the permutations of the idea, there was a knock at her door.

Kuntzler entered and in a few acidic, boozy breaths, explained that the requisition had already been filed, that they were patients in his care, and that he would personally supervise their transfer to Work Group tomorrow.

He did not hesitate to add that an armed guard would be standing outside the door to her house all evening. To protect her security in this time of transition, of course.

The guard was kind enough to listen to her. Her words, her promise, and the banded bundle of cash she placed into his hands assured that he let her and Garin pass.

Minna had difficulty moving Garin's wheelchair in a straight line. With only one arm to steer she had to lean the weight of her hips against his back and felt the heat of his body through the chair.

During the long, slow slog to Nordhausen she stopped occasionally to look up at the stars, or to kiss the tops of Garin's hands. She'd been doing so since he was an infant. He had delicate, beautiful hands, and she forced herself not to imagine the work they may have done at Maidanek. Rather she let herself feel his pulse and heat through the thin skin of her lips.

They can't have us, Garin.

All the chaos was reduced to this simple truth—the huge steel press machine in which she cradled her son was made to exert monumental amounts of pressure at an incredible speed.

This pressure had already proven its potency on flesh and bone.

That Jew died trying to destroy this thing.

Feeling the immense power of the apparatus that held her and Garin, she realized what a fool's errand it was to try and break it. Some things were too large, too immutable. There were forces around them which would not slow against resistance.

She'd toured the main floor at Nordhausen many times; she knew from watching the star-marked laborers that it took about a minute for the machine to build up to the explosive release of the vast black panel above.

Minna used that time to speak her husband's name with love.

Jakob, please forgive me. We had to escape.

She whispered kind words to her only child and ran her fingers through the still thick hair on the right side of Garin's head.

The building sound of the great machine began to fill the empty factory.

Minna was ready. She placed her lips to Garin's, closed her eyes, and waited for The Beauties to complete one last equation.

The Encore

Thirty deep black strands of hair from the bedroom carpet.

I am collecting what remains of my beautiful Zhao-shi, just days ago murdered by her defective heart.

Before her passing, Zhao-shi was capable of flight. Toured the world as part of the Dynasty Circus—The Suspended Woman. 747's her daily commute. Paris, Tokyo, London. Seldom earthbound, whether borne by flying metal behemoths or her own luxuriant hair.

Acrobats, contortionists, fire eaters—none matched her radiance.

Fifty hairs entangled in her brushes (I'd combed her hair for an hour before calling the paramedics; held my face to it, swallowed its cherry scent).

She was the girl with feather bones, floating before red backdrops, her arm-length purple-black hair tied tight to a silken blue rope, arms and legs fanned, swimming against gravity, winning. I would watch for the drift of butterfly dust crossing the stage-lights' beams.

Could I sleep, I would pray this image into my dreams.

Twenty-seven hairs from the shower drain, gently washed until they squeak.

I've been offered dope and therapy. Her friend Bai, equally confused by Zhao-shi's early death, even offered me sex as sympathy.

All are empty solace.

Seventy-two hairs on her clothes.

Zhao-shi's been dead three hundred fourteen hours as of... now.

Time will slide past like nothing, then constrict; every second is suddenly stark, cold. And *lonely* like I'd never imagined.

It's all quicksand. Just a matter of how long I can drift.

Ninety-four strands are hiding, entwined with silvery party tinsel, coiled around the motorized carpet-scrubber in our vacuum.

The tensile strength of a single hair fiber is equal to copper wire.

There's not enough left of her for a hangman's knot, but any knot will do.

The chair topples beneath me. I hover for a moment before gravity asserts itself.

Although I can't breathe, I taste the scent of cherries.

Zhao-shi holds me again.

We float home.

Consumerism

Ron, can you reach your mother from here? Yes…okay…and is she?

She is? Are you certain? And you've checked the jugular and carotid? Can you reach a mirror to check for breath signs? No.

Oh, dear…

No, son, I don't think I can move from this position right now. This shard of the bumper appears to have me pinned to the bench seat like a common Lepidoptera. You know, as a Byronic hero with a smattering of Randian objectivity flitting away in my mind, I can't help but feel disdain for this entire scenario. This is low.

Did I just call myself a Byronic hero aloud? Well then, it's out in the open. Your suspicions are quelled, correct? I'd never defined myself for you before because I felt you should find your own path and…Ugh! That is disgusting. What is that smell? Dear lord. I thought the burning gasoline was bad, but that odor…her bowels have let loose, haven't they? Death moves like quicksilver.

Ron?

Stop touching her face, Ron. Recognize death's permanency and move forward. *We* are still alive—maintaining this status should be your only focus. Let go of her hair. You and your crippling sentiment; don't give that body a value beyond what it is now.

No, it's not your mom anymore. It's water mostly, some minerals. Gases. Proteins.

Check yourself for injuries so we can assess, repair, and mobilize.

No, we should be protected if the tank explodes. You may want to breathe through your t-shirt, though. Some of that smoke *is* entering through the crack in the dashboard.

Quell that braying, Ron. Your generation...I don't understand the value you've placed in vulnerability. Were this ancient Rome you'd be of age to marry and launch an empire. Have all the pugilists retired?

What is that ticking sound? It's coming from the engine block?

Well, I paid fifty-grand for this behemoth, and I believe it will hold. Those hippies in their little tin-can cars, they used to deride me on the roadway, middle fingers held up proudly. Fools protesting survival. Proto-agrarian communists denying progress. Denying man his greatness. Imagine *their* little car flipping four times and remaining as intact as our rig. God bless military design. Sturdy as a rolling mountain. I'd have bought the version with Gatling gun intact had that been an option. Had we been that well equipped I could have gunned that possum into the troposphere...

...

Ron, I don't think I can move my head in either direction. I'll need you to get loose of your buckles and crawl back here. Ronald?

Yes, I seem to be pinned. Good God, the back of my head is a-throb...your churlish weeping isn't helping a bit, either. Silence yourself, child.

Yes, I said "child." Never believe that age alone makes a man. And don't shift about too quickly. We're still on an incline and I believe too much weight on the right side of the rig will tip us back into a roll.

...

We should never have let you drive. A possum for Pete's sake…those animals are God's litter. Furry detritus. Just an animal. Nothing. Have you ever seen *me* swerve on the roadway before?

Yes, but have you ever seen me swerve to *avoid* an animal? That's my point.

What do you think the lifespan of a possum is, anyway? How many more years of mindless foraging do you think you've assured that ball of fur by dooming us to die here in the woods?

Well, we could die. Accept that. Any given moment. Remember your cousin Dane? He was vibrant up until the second he collapsed face-first into that birthday cake. Remember how you cried that whole night. "I saw his dead eyes! I saw his dead eyes!" That was your complaint. Strange how that didn't make you wiser. Just weaker.

I really cannot feel a single one of my limbs.

I've been in and out of consciousness, haven't I? Why can't I see the trees? How long have we been here?

We've lost the final vestiges of daylight, Ron, and yet you remain there, holding her. It's so absurd. She'll begin expelling gases soon. Maybe that will loose your sad Oedipal grip and we can try to get out of here.

The burning engine was providing much of our heat, wasn't it? Funny how quickly the warmth slips away once the sun drops. I still can't command an appendage, Ron. You'll have to get moving; make a run for that tiny gas station we passed about thirty miles back. You will be Pheidippides, and I, your Athenian tribe for the saving.

Ron?

Ron?

Speak, son! I'm hoping you can reach the Mag-lite in the flip-down console. I need some light back here, and your help. I've got to assess my condition and try to stop my bleeding—there's a static fuzz to my vision so I know I'm not getting adequate circulation here, Ron...

Hello? I can see you breathing, Ron, and I doubt you're asleep. I NEED THE MAG-LITE!

Jesus, son! No need to lash out like that. Okay, so it's embedded in her chest. How was I to know that, from this vantage point? Your anger is ridiculous.

Any chance you could get a solid grip on the light and free it for our use? I bet one solid tug would do the job.

Ron?

Ron?

It was my hubris, I suppose, to think us so invincible in this vehicle. Should I have packed flares? Yes, that's obvious. Water? Yes, even more obvious.

Perhaps, Ron, there's an errant package of Fritos on the floor near me. A Snak-Pak, maybe?

But this machine did keep us alive. I had to have it at first sight, this shining example of man's command over nature; our bodies reshaping steel, our minds designing perfect geometric infrastructures, our wills dredging liquid fire from the Earth's belly and converting it into unprecedented levels of speed, striking down drudgery and demanding progress.

And don't start, Ron, with your sniping. How you ever developed your line of leftist drivel while being home-schooled, I'll never know. The fact is that it is best to consume everything we can, while we can. Sustainability is a fantasy for those believing that humans were meant to exist forever as they are now—LIES!

I have never known such a level of thirst…Ron? I swear there was an extra Snak-Pak up near the driver's seat. Maybe some aspirin? This headache's gone thermonuclear.

We have to use up all the oil, Ron. It's what our bodies do. We consume. And when we are done consuming one thing, our bodies will learn to ingest another and our lights shall burn forever on. So said Darwin. So said Emerson—the conflict defines us. Ether and stardust swirling, colliding, sparking off into new shapes. If you had your way, we'd be stagnating on some insect-riddled farm right now, fondling possums and plucking fiddles while our teeth rot.

Oh…my head…

Well…dead ship captains on mosquito ponds, Ron! We'll not return to the stew. That doesn't match up on a theological or biological level. That's not why we're here…

Parched does not begin to define how I'm feeling here, Ron.

Your dad always wanted to be a poet, kiddo. I aspired, but aspiration was all that was within my reach. Playground injury, Ron. Age eight. Flew off the swings inverted, caught my head on the plywood marking the park's border.

The doctors never defined this clearly, Ron, but I believe that that *exact* moment was when I lost my grip on meter.

Pieces of you, Ron, they can die at a whim.

Especially, Ron, especially if you can't get your fucking whimpering little cur bitch of a son to bring you a GODDAMNED MOTHERFUCKING FRITO SNAK-PAK!

Your punishment, son…yes, your *punishment*, for even in this situation you must understand that all of life is a lesson, and you're lucky to have your elder to guide you…your punishment now shall be to understand survival. Basic animal survival…the way to soothe the reptilian bits at the back of your medulla so that you may live past this moment and continue to ascend to your higher human calling.

So wake up. Yes, that's it. Look me in the eyes, like a man.

The sun is rising. Your dark night of the soul is over, Ron, and you have to move forward.

Crawl back here. Carefully. Slowly. Keep the vehicle in balance. Your right leg looks dreadful, but it doesn't appear the femoral artery's been cut. That's good. That's good. You can do this, Ron. You can take your punishment and grow up strong.

Smell my breath, Ron. That tint to it, the thing worse than morning breath, that fresh cat-shit smell…that's me dying. And I can tell by the look in your eyes that my assessment is correct. I'm missing crucial human elements, aren't I?

Well, I could tell by the buzzing of flies at dawn, by the soft prickle of their landings in wide perimeter, that the rear of my skull is perhaps missing. I sense a gulf of tissue.

That bad, is it? The idea of me seeing another sunset with that much of my brain exposed to the elements is absurd. So it is that you, my only seed, must carry on as I instruct.

You can survive this, Ron. You are, at this moment, only an organism. And you must consume. Fluids, proteins. And if the Iroquois were right, perhaps a bit of my strength.

I proffer this now, the flesh of the father. Let my mind give you life. It is my last wish. It is your duty.

Tilt my head forward more? Perhaps that bit of glass by my feet will help you serrate….

Yes, you can do it. You must. Move swiftly, that this throbbing may abate and I may catch up with your mother at the soft, light gates of her heaven.

And gently at first, please…yes, that's it…please stop crying...no more sentiment…you are an animal now, and must remain so until you return to the world of man… oh, to be part of this Greek tragedy, it feels right, a poet's end…I am your Leonidas, eat well for you may not survive the day…yes, dig in…I'll not ask you to describe the taste… to paraphrase Joplin I suggest you take another little piece… Gorp! I can't…oh, God, a bit of blood in my eyes, I can't see much…your hands are stronger than I'd imagined them to be…how I love and despise you, Ron…yes, burrow in, son, let your throat be gorged with my wisdom, swallow ages of evolution…oops, you've got a bit on your chin there, tut-tut, no waste in nature…they were right—there's no pain, no self-aware nerves in the gray matter itself…aaaaooooaahh… that last scoop touched off an old memory—the smell of the Atlantic in mid-winter New England, a hint of your mother's perfume…but what is this light…Oh, holy fire! Yes, Ron. I will live on through you…in you…carry on, consume, survive…swallow me down, Ron…take me deep, child, and become a man….

Wall of Sound:
A Movement in Three Parts

Entrance

Right at the fucking kick-off, I've got to ask you to do something you're not going to want to do.

I've got one issue before we go any further.

It's that friend you've brought with you; the friend who always carries you through darker times like this; the one who helps you wake up in the morning; the one who feeds you breakfast and better aspirations; the one who makes tomorrow seems like a birthday cake filled with cash.

Yeah, *that* friend.

You're going to have to kill him.

End him.

Push him to the ground and crack his mouth wide open; slide his teeth onto the curb until you hear enamel chipping against Reddi-Mix pavement. Start stomping.

Kill your friend. It's for your own good.

If somebody like *that* ever stepped foot in here, *in a place like this*, they'd chew a fucking hole through *you* to escape. He takes one step over this threshold, you won't survive.

I'm not the bad guy here. I'm a realist. And I'm asking you to do me a favor.

Just one favor, and we can proceed...

I. BURN/Liquidation

"E-bomb?"

"Yeah, right here, yo," drops out of my mouth in response, even though I promised just about everybody I know I would go straight for a while, and even though my serotonin levels are so dangerously low I'm too depressed to even bother to kill myself, and even though, and this strikes me as particularly fucked, the kid dealing looks a lot like the old bearded Christ, and smells of cold beef and paint thinner.

The stinky guy scopes over his shoulders, digs the scene. Digs on me, a very long, sly look. He's not gay, just clockin' to make sure I'm not El Narco Federali. He checks out my gigantic denims, the tattoos, the sunken eyes, sunken chest, sunken general demeanor, makes his assessment.

"What you need, dog?" rolls out of his mouth, low and greasy sounding over his thin, chewed on lips. Damn! Breath like hot turpentine on this guy. Flash second passes, I wonder if he's dealing to support a hardcore paint huffer habit, but then I check myself. Those types are so low rent they could never get up the capital to start dealing. Spend half their fucking time with "Gold Glitter" Dacryl spray paint flecked on their mugs, vomit in their hair. You get near them and you can smell the burning brain cells and hear the sizzle in the cerebellum, the screams of the million vanquished bits of gray matter. Huffing is like a fucking Personal Mental Genocide Program. Is that a band name? Probably. I bet...

BUY THE PILLS AND TAKE THEM!

I've got a vicious mental drift problem, so I have to force myself to focus. Get the drug, the drug is what matters here.

The e-bomb, MDMA, ecstasy. Definitely more important. Get, acquire, consume, start the party, put the jumper cables to the old kicker for one more stretch of beats and dancing. Dig on the lasers. Stinky Christ is getting impatient with my spacey behavior, so I ask, "Got any Mitsubishis of Apple-jacks?" Dependable old favorites.

"Nah, man, nah, you don't want that shit, that shit is old, *old* old, played out," he says, slow, with emphasis on the fact that my favorite drugs are now "old old" which I guess is about as old as shit can get these days. "Nah, for twenty-five I can get you these double stack Karaoke e-bombs, or you can try the new shit."

My first reflection is this—Do I want to play guinea pig for some backwoods chemist?

Second reflection—Is this bitch-looking doper just trying to pass his bunk goods off on me so he can give his quality pills to his regular customers?

Third—Is looking like Jesus a real aesthetic choice, or just something that happens to skinny white kids that don't take care of themselves, hygiene-wise?

Fourth—Why am I talking to this flipped out Christ cat when the party is really starting to go off. Especially when I could be right up by the main speakers catching some bass-waves and putting some moves on that blonde doll with the pink hair and translucent angel wings?

Final reflection—None. Thoughtless. Urgency and impulse kick in, thought replaced by need for the pill, the pleasure, and now, now, now, NOW, *NOW!*

"Yeah, lemme see the new stuff, yo." As Stinky Christ pulls his little knit (from hemp, I'm positive) satchel out from under his natty jacket I wonder when I started talking this stupid.

Ending sentences with "yo" cannot sound good or reflect on me positively, in any way. Not even in a smirking ironic asshole kind of way. I have to squat to get to my secret pocket hidden on the inner, upper right leg of my big-ass pants.

I pull out a little wad of cash, a couple of twenties and eight one dollar bills, which I will spend later on bottles of water to be consumed almost perpetually throughout the night. I have "The Dehydration" brand of drug fear, ecstasy and coke specific. The quantity and frantic quality of my e-bomb generated dance moves causes me to sweat in profusion, and I'm not sure of all the details, but I heard some shit once about liver necrosis and electrolyte washout that sounded crazy ill. Of course, on the flipside I heard about the roller who drank so much fucking water he got hydrotoxification, and died from drinking *too much* water. I only bring in eight bucks, so that I drink a lot, but don't drink so much that my body bloats like a loofah.

I unroll the twenties, make a final scope for John Law or those steroid sucking pricks that run security for these parties, and make my purchase. In the Unkempt Dealer's hand, forty bucks. In mine, two clear gel caps filled with an unknown yellow and black powder.

Quick thought. "Yo, what's in these, dog?"

The skinny kid is all smile, more of an Aum Shinrikyo smile than a Loving Savior smile. "You're gonna dig it. Some pure MDMA, some DMT, and little bit of mutant type-A streptococcus. I call 'em Roman Candles. They light you up and blow you the fuck out, *yo*. Peace. If you like 'em, tell your friends. I'm the ice cream man."

Funny guy, stepping up to me with that copped "yo" shit, and he has the nerve to tell me he put bacteria in my drugs.

HA HA HA, that's one class act sense of humor you've got there, you fucking jerk. Laugh it up. Back in the day I would have rolled him, but now I have to kick all this peace, love, unity, and respect shit, so I walk away, towards the beats and the girls. I'm thinking, for some reason, "I'm a bigger dumb-ass than that guy."

Backlash for the violent thoughts. I've done too many drugs to play tough any more. Spell it, B-U-R-N-O-U-T. No one constant emotion, no steady thoughts.

Kicking out the rave-style stroll now, part dance/part walk. Big bounce in my step, head nodding with the four on the floor basswaves being dropped by DJ Northern Light. The music is percussive, tight and jazzy. Standard bass, snare, and cymbal House arrangement, with some nice distorted bass arpeggios under it, and every third measure there's a fat keyboard stab. I'm feeling it, locked into the beat and I'm not even rolling yet. Best to play cool early, bust out a couple of dance moves, but don't get crazy. I have to save that for when everybody is high, because, ugly truth be told, I'm not the tightest dancer and I know my moves will better represent to those who are deeply and chemically fucked. If you get high enough you can watch a guy wearing a Winnie the Pooh backpack slowly spinning some glow sticks on strings, and actually think, "WOW! I am genuinely amazed at this display of talent! Hooray for this!" Which, I'm sober enough to recognize right now, is fucking ridiculous.

I go up by the speakers and scope out the party. Buzzed, majorly buzzed now, just off the music, and maybe the presence of so many girls who I know will never ask me for commitment. The right kinds of girls treat me like a party favor. They use me, then the party's over, lights go up, the drugs wear off, and I'm discarded along with the no longer glowing plastic tubes, unwanted flyers, empty water bottles, and countless wads of bubble gum.

Which is fine by me. I don't really need them as long as I've got the drugs.

JESUS H., MAN. YOU ARE A FUCKING BURNOUT! Listen to yourself.

Yeah, I better reprioritize soon, but I have parties laid out for at least the next three months. I'll get on that priority shit later, yo.

No worries. No unnecessary judgment of self. Every once in awhile my conscience likes to kick thoughts up without asking me to think them first. Like Jiminy Cricket with no Goddamn tact.

"I fucking hate myself," I'm thinking, and suddenly, too suddenly. If I'm not bi-polar, I'm working on it. I try to ignore the thought, feel the music, close my eyes and move. The place is too hot, the venue sucks, and although I like DJ Northern Light I'm not vibing off the House any more. I want some Speed Garage, some Jungle, even some Happy Hardcore, anything that will push me harder, push out the thought, make me just feel.

Time to hit up the Roman Candles.

I'm hating this party so bad I decide to give myself a good, brutal brainfuck, and I slip *both* of the pills into my hand. They sit there in the soft, lazy flesh of my hand, and they feel warm. The lasers above my head reflect dimly off the smooth gelcaps. I get a big, fat smile, and I'm thinking (or maybe just feeling), "Yeah, here we go!"

As I lift the pills to my mouth I hesitate for one tiny moment as I feel both of the e-bombs shift unexpectedly in my hand, like Mexican jumping beans. "Come on dumbfuck, there are no insects in your pills. Goddamn burnout! Eat 'em!"

Down the tubes, and it feels like they shift inside my throat too. I shouldn't

have dry swallowed. Secondary gag reflex, then it passes.

Downtime. I'm waiting for the pills to kick. I've had DMT before and I'm starting to hope there's not too much in these Roman Candles, but done is done. I saw a guy on T.V. once who could purposefully regurgitate any item he swallowed, be it car keys, marbles, whole eggs, prophylactics, whatever. I do not possess this skill, so the pills will remain in my belly. Swimming in the nervous acid.

I'm really starting to sketch on the DMT, hoping I won't see God, or cherubim, or anything too otherworldly. People who see that type of shit have a tendency to forget to breathe. I'm a lifetime respirator. Breathing is life. I love feeling my lungs expand, sucking in the air.

Shit, now I'm thinking on it too much; I've become aware of my breathing. I have to mentally contract my diaphragm. I have to will each breath. In and out, in and out, try to circular breathe, in through the nose, hold three seconds, out through the mouth. In three, hold three, out three, the magic three. Focused. Relaxing. Let the autonomic system take over, you dumb bastard.

The percussive waves pushing through the room speed up, gaining the steady stomp of sixteenths. Nice. The DJ just segued into some Hardcore. Yeah, I'm feeling this. I start walking around, spying the mean-ass grimaces on the people's collective faces, diggin' it big time. Hands in the air, frantic limbs twisting, heads really bopping, sweat dripping, some peoples eyes closing, just really *feeling it*. My nervousness assuages a little, mellows out, although I briefly get the *What If This Hallucinogen Makes Me Claw My Fucking Eyes Out Because I Think I Can Never Come Down* fear.

It is a valid fear; I've seen the fallout of a bad trip before.

Two years ago, at a house party in Eugene, I saw a girl trip so hard on her own mug in the mirror that she flipped permanent-style. She'd been staring at her face for too long, maybe five minutes, and then she started brushing her teeth with someone's old, blue toothbrush, the kind with the little red rubber thing at the end that looks like a perfect chocolate chip. She murmured something about circles, and something else about her never being clean again, none of us ever being clean, and then she started scrubbing her teeth. No water involved in this, just a big glob of Aquafresh Whitening and that old plastic hygiene utensil. The look on her face was so intense I had to bail, even though the bathroom was the one quiet place in the party where a kid could really just bug out on shit. Anyway, a few minutes later I'm out on the back porch, seeing purple eyeballs in the sky and all that, and I hear a girl inside screaming these awful, wet screams. Typically good blotter renders me mad coward, but I charged into the house anyway.

Mistake. In the living room, backed into the corner, was my toothbrush girl. The front of her white tank top was covered in red and white, blood and toothpaste foam. Her right hand was wrapped like a claw around the brush and the plastic bristles had been flattened. Her fingers, the utensil, and her face were all soaking crimson. Her mouth was a big black hole, oozing blood over her lower lip and down her neck, where some of it had already coagulated, thick like jelly, in the hollow of her throat. She looked like a trapped animal, deeply sad, deeply scared, and most of all confused.

She looked around the room, and then she dropped the toothbrush. Backed against the corner, she sunk to the floor, slow, face oozing bubbly red paste. My brain and my stomach flipped, and I darted outside, knowing that nothing good was going to happen in that room. Out on the deck I heard her start to sob, and sort of scream at the same time. "Mommy, mommy, uagghh, I, I, I'm cleeeeeaaaann now! Clean!"

I vomited on the way to my car, smelled Chicken Noodle Soup, spilled beer, copper pennies and bile. I was too high to drive, but way, way too high to be anywhere near that nightmare. Too much ill shit. Too much reality. Too much of a fucking After School Special "Tragic Moment of the Week." I hope I never bug like that, but they don't call DMT "The Rocketship" due to its lack of effectiveness, so I have to focus, remember that nobody trips forever, except for schizos and Italian film directors.

"So," I think to myself, "what's the agenda, old sport, old chum, pally of mine?" I can't answer, figuring that it is kind of too late to do any planning, knowing that I just have to go along with the ride, check the vibe, maybe dance a little later, when the bomb really hits. Maybe, a couple of hours after that, find a girl, whatever, just to talk, maybe a little more. Maybe find some "buddies" doing coke. It's amazing how fast I can become close friends with somebody I spy chopping out some fat, white rails. The duration of the friendship usually lasts from the moment I find out they have coke, to the moment I start tasting that nasty, acetone-type drip.

Then I run away. I actually run sometimes. Fucking tweeker. I simply cannot be trusted.

I decide to kick around the party some more, purchase some water, enough to keep me hydrated for at least an hour. I hang on for an extra second at the bar, hoping to catch a little lingering eye contact with the hottie in the silk looking haltertop with the Japanese/Chinese/Taiwanese/Pekinese/etc. symbol on it. She's too busy, no go. Fuck it, just keep moving. Pondering the current club kid fetish with all things Eastern, wondering how many kids out there are tattooed and variously adorned with Asian symbols that don't mean what the kids think. Like my friend Perry, the dumbfuck gets a huge, black and green tattoo of a Japanese kanji symbol between his shoulder blades. Guy at the shop told him it means "courage." Two weeks later an exchange student from Daihatsu or wherever spies Perry by the Olympic size pool at the university, asks him why he has the word "eggplant" tattooed on his back. Perry was crazy pissed. Too ashamed to do anything about it, though. He trusted the lousy biker fuck at the shop, and now, barring any highly expensive laser surgery, he will spend the rest of his life proudly festooned with the word EGGPLANT in bold ink on flesh.

I decide it's time to dig on some Jungle, and at thinking this I suddenly get this deep, blood-level urge to hear some hard, dark, rapid beats. I really need it. The power of self-suggestion renders me frantic.

I see kids headed down a narrow staircase towards, I hope and pray, some sort of Jungle DJ room. Shit, I didn't even check the flyer. I never do anymore. What if there's no fucking Jungle, just a bunch of Goddamn sissy ass disco-fuck booty fucking House? Fucking useless, prancy worthless disco redux bullshit!

Whoa! Whoa there, boy! Just feeling the speed of my drugs kicking in. Check pulse, verify it as way above average. Need some beats to match it. Jungle definitely, maybe even some Breakbeat. Need audio saturation, waves upon waves, the old Phil Spector Wall of Sound.

I push my old Vans down the staircase, stepping around two fucking e-tards who clearly took their pills way too early and will probably be lying dazed and sedate in each others arms by three in the morning. The two are making out crazy fierce, sweat pouring down both of them, hips smashed together, tongues playing. Just for a moment I start to jones, then I remember, "I'm here for the music, for the party." Still, it looks like a real thrill ride. I probably wouldn't have the easiest time playing pick-up with all this DMT that's supposedly in my system, anyway. Waiting for it to hit, tick...tock...I want to be interstellar high in the next twenty minutes, I'm ready. I hit the bottom floor.

"This DJ is really punishing, man!" says the candy kid at the base of the stairs. I can't focus, the room is too hot, way too dank, and I'm sure that with each breath I'm sucking down a couple of liters of other people's vaporized sweat. These beats are so distorted, I can't even figure out what's spinning. Shit, the walls are tight, no room to dance. I'll probably pass out if I spend one more moment in here.

Fuck it, I'm heading back up topside. Out of this moist little cavity, this bacterial barn filled with kids too high to notice just how *nasty* it is in here. I pass the e-tard couple on the way back up. Christ, it looks like a conjugal visit. As I roll by I say, "Yo, the Olympic Dry Humping Team try-outs are next week. Damn!" It sounded kind of clever in the split second where I generated the thought and decided to speak it, but as it's coming out of my mouth I can't help feeling oafish, gawky, and weird. I guess I get kind of bitchy when I'm waiting for pills to kick.

I head back into the main room, which is now definitely where it is at. The kid up top is still spinning Hardcore, some real rough, *You Are All Going To Be Killed By Giant Robots Owned By Multi-National Corporations* kind of Hardcore, with distortion that is just ripping my face off. I scope around, see kids sitting down already. Probably whacked some ketamine, forgot how to move. Dumb.

I'm trying to dance, starting to hop a little bit, getting the arms into it, putting on a big smile. Problem is, the Hardcore, combined with the rising sensation of being vaguely high is just making me mean. I feel like throwing up a fist or something, some kind of Slayer concert aggression. Knowing that any particular type of testosterone induced behavior would be frowned upon amidst this neutered "New Disco" set, I chill and head up towards the front to watch the DJ. Maybe he's really cutting it up.

Here at the front of the room the DJ is oblivious to his audience. He seems to be concentrating on one knob on the mixer in particular, although with each of his manipulations I hear no actual change in the track. Wanker DJ style, making dramatic motions for the crowd while in actuality afraid to really mess with the mix, and make the song his own. Timid DJ's deserve no credit. The records are spinning fast, the BPM on the mixer looks outrageous, and it looks like one of the records is by an artist called "Darkstep" which for some reason puts a feeling of terror in my belly. I realize I have about five seconds before my Rocketship takes off, the vibe is rising like electric waves. My nerves are acid tight and I can feel a strange burn just under the skin, like you get from eating too much niacin before a tox screen.

Finally, here we are. Highsville, USA.

Population: Me.

Mad pressure behind my eyes, like my systolic and diastolic just found out they were going to have an unwanted baby. I hope my blood pressure isn't swelling the veins on my neck and forehead because it makes me look like the fucking devil, and I'm still thinking of getting my mack on, or at least finding a girl to get a back rub from, if I get too bugged out. Tingling on my scalp, like that "egg crack" thing kids used to do on top of each others heads back in second grade.

For one moment everything in my peripheral stops moving, like painted walls close on each side of me, and then, a moment later everything moves into top speed, playing catch up. Big grin from me, face spread tight, too happy, almost like a rictus, a grimace. Unnatural happy, like I can't shake it. Fuck it, even a overbearingly dumb grin is better than the typical hallucinogen addled expression a.k.a. The Zoned Out Space Case Look. The empty "I just whacked back a brick of dusted cat tranquilizer and now I don't know where I am, who I am, or how to move/ Dawn of the Dead" type look.

I don't ever want to rock that style, and shit, now I'm thinking about zombies, ashen faces, bloody toothbrushes, etc. Which is bad under normal circumstances and tragic on DMT so I rush over to a speaker bank to try and clean my brain out. The good old Sonic Chimney Sweep.

Concentrate on the beats, focus, hear the layers, don't think in circles. I grab the speaker grill right in front of one of the bass reflex areas, feel the waves, the warm air expelled across my forehead feels perfect, like a light breeze on a sunny day. I close my eyes and there's swirling sunshine trapped beneath the lids, shifting, bright, with little purple and green bubbles in it. YES. The breeze from the speaker is giving me full body tingles, every inch is pulled tight, every tiny little hair on my head, my arms, the back of my neck is feeling the basslines, and I want to throw my head back in some sort of exaltation, but I fear that any tiny movement will alter the body high.

How long can I stand here like this, mated to the goddamn speaker? How long before some coked-out little candy raver tries to give me some Vicks? How long before I get bumped into? How long until some concerned little rave citizen asks me if I'm okay, do I need some water, or some gum, or something? Which of course I don't need, and yes I'm perfectly okay, unbelievably okay right here in my little e-tard womb, as long as nobody messes with me.

I am content, and I imagine that this is what people who achieve Zen feel like, and then realize that if it is, I've really cheated my way into it. Forty dollars for perfect Zen. What a great fucking deal! Wait, I can feel eyes on me now. Bad eyes watching. What? Oh, don't let me get the Fear, I'm like praying to whoever is up there and presides over tripped out little guys who get in too deep. Re-focus, catch the music again, trap it inside my head. New agenda: MOVE!

I can't.

Which is bad.

Which is so very fucking *deeply bad.*

Um, oh shit, oh shit, oh shit. Move, move move move move move!

This feels wrong. My eyes won't open. I know my heart is beating, I can feel it in my neck, along the carotid and jugular, and I must be breathing, although I can't feel much shift in my chest.

MOVE! My body is not receiving commands. Fucking synapses aren't connecting or something.

A new body high hits me. Right up my spine, sharp. Strychnine? No, not an option, don't overthink, don't panic. *MOVE!* A new skin tingle, like tacks being shot into me, then melting away. Not painful, but bad. Maybe. *PLEASE MOVE!* Shit, this is hazy. I keep fading my thoughts out. Just as I almost have one, really grasp it and think it, it blasts away with my pulse. *PLEASE JUST MOVE! ANYTHING! DON'T FREEZE LIKE THIS!*

Across my arms I feel these alien tickles, like insect motion, and I can't brush it away. Then it whips through my arms, up the front of my chest (am I breathing?) and surges up behind my eyelids, pregnant with unwanted visions. In front of my eyes there is some kind of tapestry, seventies style, lots of pastels, paisley, some ornate horse drawings. Yes, definitely horses, with dark black scales. Fucking...what... lizard horses? *MOVE!* This is not good. I don't like this. I can't control this. The lizard horses start to run, black scales dropping off their rib cages, exposing dark blue liquid innards. They are charging away from me, hooves kicking up purple spots that rotate and smash into each other as they speed by my head, wherever *that* is. *JUST FUCKING MOVE NOW!* Just a toe, or an eyelid, or my feet or something. Maybe I'm okay. No. Can't remain inactive. Why can't I hear anything? Where did the music go?

Then.............BAM!.............and the music screams back into my head, my eyes pop open. OhthankGod! Eyes under control, move something else. I shift my head up slowly, it feels dense, and there's more pressure behind my eyes, like weights stitched to the optic nerve, seeking the ground. I want to get to the restroom, throw some water on my face, maybe sit down further away from the music. Oh shit, my hands burn. I must have been smashing them into the speaker grates. I peep at them, and know I must be out-of-my-noggin fried, because it looks like they are bleeding, like the speaker grates sunk right into them, the criss-cross pattern pushed into my skin. I recall the sage old Geto Boys, realize my mind must be playing tricks on me. It really looks likes I'm bleeding though. Fuck it, even if it is real I'll just suffer the wound, and remember not to press against the grate so hard next time. I head towards the restroom.

Everyone I walk past seems made of plastic, even though they are moving. Like little machines, each engineered for one specific task. Look, there's the machine that hops up and down, and over there is the little thing that just nods its head, and there's the good old "passed out in a puddle of his own vomit" machine, and to my left is the "chewing holes through her own cheeks because she forgot the fucking bubblegum and is clearly remiss about it, and doesn't know quite what to do" machine, and by the wall we have the "stretching-its-calves" machine, number 112558.

My little world, everyone else is plastic.

Shove my hands in my pocket, and they really do hurt, sharply. Damn. I'm probably bleeding all over my sixty dollar denims. As I walk away the DJ looks sinister, hunched over the decks like he has some kind of weapon inside and he is just waiting for the perfect time to unleash it. Diabolical DJ and his Sinister Set.

I have taken some very bad pills, and I would now like some help, some comfort, some anything but this. I've got it bad now, The Fear, but I've had it before, and I can ride it out.

How? I'm surrounded by machines. Bits of plastic, minds of silicon/carbon composite. The floor feels like it is yielding too much. Quicksand? Picturing: slow death, no one reaching in to help me out, water and sand down my gullet, in my eyes. Out think this, damn it! Get to the bathroom.

I finally get to the restroom door, or rather it rushes up to meet me after a few confused and nauseous moments of staggering, and as I head in I remember one of my rules, which is to never go near mirrors while tripping. Monsters in there, monsters in me. I flush water into my face, turn away from the mirror and dig on two shirtless guys, absolutely glitter-soaked, licking each other's hands. E-tard shit is almost enough to make me smile, but something seems desperate about their passion, empty, and besides, I've suddenly realized I need to piss.

I push past the licking buddies and into the bowels of the restroom, which is, of course, already flooding, and reeks of vomit.

Focus, unbutton my pants. Say howdy to the unit, give it the ol' wink like " 'Ello there, chap." I can feel pressure in my bladder, but the urine won't flow. Staring at the wall in front of me, I spy a fucking old, green booger somebody was clever enough to smear there. There is a thick black nostril hair caked into it, with a crusty white follicle hanging pendulously at its end. My eyes can feel the weight at the base of the follicle, the slight urgings of gravity versus the co-efficient of friction that holds the follicle and hair firmly to the snot. I'm seeing in too much detail. The wall suddenly seems forty feet away; the trip is distorting my depth perception. I don't want to force a piss, but there will be people waiting behind me soon, and the muffled sound of the beats is somehow scary in this florescent lit little hole. I look down at my dick again, try to visualize myself urinating. Like coach said, "Picture it inside your head and then make it happen." There we go. It's warm, too warm and sort of burning. More bad, just more and more bad from these pills.

"If I fucking find that dealer..." I think, but the pain at the head of my unit stops me from even thinking. I look down and see that the tail end of my stream of urine is rose colored. Shit. Blood from my hands? No. More and more bad, and now my dick feels like it's on fire, like somebody opened up my urethra and jammed in a habanero pepper. My hands are bloody waffles and now I might have an STD or some shit. I've got to sit down and just drown out the world until this trip ends.

I'm wondering if the e-bomb is going to accentuate my current pain as much as it used to accentuate the pleasure. I shiver, shove my hands into my pockets, and head back out, body on fire from the inside.

People are looking at me.

All of them.

Even the people with their eyes closed. I can feel it, waves of paranoia, sticking to me like molasses. The room smells like fried meat now, and aftershave. Mixed signals everywhere have me scared, twitching and tweeking. I spot the PartySmart table and stagger over, thinking I can ask them for help or something. The PartySmart group shows up at the parties and tries to encourage kids to abstain from drugs (or at least use them wisely), provides information on safer drug use, and offers free candy, condoms, and other miscellaneous well-intended services. As far as their actual effectiveness they are kind of the equivalent of a band-aid over a cancer sore. They don't do much, but it's nice to have them there. It looks better, PR-wise.

At the table there are flyers with information about drugs I've never even heard of before, or maybe I've heard of them under different names. Blood of a Wig, Morning Glory Seeds, and Datura? What? Doesn't matter. Focus, come down, get help.

A kid with a blue goatee and a Rainbow Brite visor on sees me, and says something, but I can't understand what he says, through my panic. Sounds like maybe he said, "Treble morph de dealy whopper, man." It doesn't matter. Nothing else matters in light of what my eyes just focused on. I'm staring at the light blue flyer taped to the fake wood surfacing, and my heart is about to explode.

It's right there, and I touch it, real as day, I can feel the paper fibers, see the black ink lightly reflecting the pulse of a far off strobe. Too real, in bold print.

"WARNING—DO NOT PURCHASE DRUGS FROM THIS MAN. HE IS A KNOWN FELON, AND HAS SOLD HIGHLY DANGEROUS AND POTENTIALLY LETHAL DRUGS DURING AT LEAST THREE PARTIES IN THE LAST YEAR. HE IS A MEMBER OF THE NEO-NAZI GROUP KNOWN AS 'THE LIGHTNING REICH' WHICH HAS BEEN SPECIFICALLY TARGETING THE RAVE COMMUNITY FOR HATE CRIMES. IF YOU SEE THIS INDIVIDUAL PLEASE IMMEDIATELY ALERT LOCAL AUTHORITIES, OR LET SOMEONE AT PARTYSMART KNOW! THANKS, P.L.U.R."

Underneath the text, ugly as when I met him, is the one-and-only Stinky Christ, my chosen-at-random dealer for tonight's little get together. His name is apparently "Morton Greens," although that has to be an alias. I just can't imagine a Nazi I could call "Morty" for short. Less facial hair, but still definitely him, definitely, and I think I can smell him, even through the picture. I need to throw up, and the PartySmart kid can tell something is wrong with me. I'm probably five shades of white right now, but I can't talk, I have to run away. To anywhere else. This is too real.

On the way into the main area I run into a door and my left hand leaves a smear of red, still oozing blood. I can feel the head of my dick, one hundred percent on fire now, like how I imagine a steam burn would feel, and I might be crying. Things are blurry, the music is too loud, relentless. I'm confused, fumbling, trying to think about the Stinky Christ, trying to convince myself that I'm having a deeply bad trip and that in reality I'm probably just curled up in a corner somewhere, shaking, but the pain is too real, too sharp. How could that guy be a Nazi? He had so much hair! Nazis can't have hair! Shit, everything I'm trying to dig on is so blurry. Not a dream, my guts are fucking burning, really, incontrovertibly burning. I've eaten poison. My heart is going so fast now I can't even differentiate beats, panic through my whole chest.

Then I look around, and see hell, only this hell comes equipped with lasers, and strobes, and disco balls, and beats, which is all somehow much worse than a traditional fire and brimstone brand of hell.

Kids everywhere are doubled over; the one closest to me has a string of bloody vomit hanging from his lip. It looks like his little plastic necklace is sinking into his neck, scraping into his trachea. What did Stinky Christ a.k.a. "Morton Greens" feed us? Flashback on his joke, "...mutant streptococcus..."

NOT A JOKE! FUCKING SHIT!

My ankles roll out from under me. The floor is carpeted but I feel the concrete slap right into my skull. My skull gives too much, crusted red hands reach up and bring back new, wet blood. I can barely do it, but I shift my head across the ground, crane my neck, and see *him* behind the DJ booth.

It has to be him, fucking "Morton Greens" wearing an old World War II gas mask now, along with his hippie "camouflage," grabbing the live P.A. microphone. It's clear he wants to speak, but he seems to be having trouble finding the right switch with that mask on. I don't want to hear his voice, I just want a fucking ambulance, some help, anything.

Oh shit, "Morton Greens" found the switch.

The proud Aryan brothers of the Lightning Reich have a message to deliver to those of our race who seek to escape their duty...

What duty?! Fucking vapid Nazi bullshit, man! My head is throbbing, it feels thick, heavy, and loose on my neck, like if I move it any more my head will separate from my neck, accompanied by the sound of tearing paper.

Oh, God, please let me come out of this, I'm done tripping, done tripping, give me back control, fuck all these drugs, fuck Nazis and turntables and giant pants and stillborn relationships based on mutual drug abuse.

...to the Great White Crusade, to The Cause. Those of you before me this evening are suffering because you seek escape from the responsibility of our great brotherhood.

You will die tonight because you chose to.

You will die tonight...

Fuck the candy kids with fake angel wings and candy jewelry and even all the beats. Fuck all this bullshit and give me back my life and take away this pain.

Let me wake up.

Nobody is listening. "Come on," I'm thinking, as I see security rushing around, as freaked out kids step over my body in a rush to the door, "I repent, man, let me come out of this." My head feels like it is burning now too, and I can't see anything anymore. I try to open my eyes. I have to see, have to crawl to help. I reach up gingerly to open my eyelids with my fingers and the tissue has too much give. Too much pain everywhere in my body, I didn't even feel my eyes rupture. They are soft in the sockets, like warm, wet, rotten little peaches. In my right eye socket my finger pushes up against the lens itself, hard yet yielding like a Superball, and now I feel the pain there…

...because you and your regressive and pagan behavior are contributing to the weakening of our race. The members of the Lightning Reich have decided that you race traitors have contributed to our decline long enough. Now, we are cleaning up the mess, before the next generation is affected by your weakness, your ignorance, and your lack of desire for true societal advancement according to the rules laid out by The Turner Diaries.

Enjoy your last trip.

…and the top of my head is burning white hot, like an insanely *sharp* ache somehow, the whole head feeling rotten and close to caving with each throb, and "Morton Greens" seems to have stopped talking, and now I can hear screams, too many screams, too many of them pitched up ridiculously high, like the squeals and bleats of the slaughterhouse my aunt took me by when I was eight, and it feels like maybe my guts just spilled out, but I'm too afraid to reach down and feel, I just want to wake up, and I think God's a real bastard for allowing me to trip this hard, oh please let this all be a trip, and someone is screaming for their daddy across the room, and I want to cry but my eyes exploded so I just scream and scream, and realize that the DJ likely ran from the building but he left the albums spinning, and I can feel the beats through the floor, vibrating my flesh and quickly rendering it into something less and less substantive, and I'm hoping now that if this is real I will die, and soon, and I'm also thinking, somewhere much further off, "Welcome to my After School Special," and I want to laugh, but my throat just dripped to the floor,

and

I

cannot

breathe.

Passage

Of course, there's more to it than just that, than just the suffering, the screaming.

There are worse circles I could have shown you. Places where the physical doesn't even have a chance to manifest. Places with razor-filled wombs, acidic air.

Places with nothing at all.

I could have left you there.

But you did me that favor. You abandoned your friend at the door, and with quite a bit of gusto.

How did you know your fist would fit down his throat?

No response? That's okay. You've seen a lot today.

Best to remain quiet, even as we leave this place. You don't belong here with these charred remains. But mistakes have been made before. Quicksand seldom pushes people back up to the air.

So let's move quickly, eh?

This next place were headed to, it's almost as bad. Worse, in my opinion. Hope can be torture.

The people here, they think they've got a fucking chance to get out, to move up to the next level.

Sometimes I come here just to watch them. Just to laugh.

II. PURGE/Deeper

1 deep

[mdma/dextromethorphan/methamphetamine]

and I'm still feeling everything (too much) and I'm waiting, with a bitter taste at the back of my mouth like a whisper, its soft voice promising "*Things will improve.*" Tick tock tick tock tick tock... my heart beat is faster, but good odds say it's psychosomatic (shit, if I could get a psychosomatic high all the time I wouldn't need to eat this poison every weekend; just a clean placebo buzz burning through my system).

So the DJ bombs us with bass and everything is BOOM-BOOM-BOOM-BOOM (God, it's got to be easy to produce trance, house, techno, jungle, any of it, just turn on the drum machine and strap a monkey to it, then hook that monkey up to an amphetamine drip, teach it to twist knobs, tap buttons, nod head with meaning) BOOM (no variety *please*, it might upset these regressive e-tards, any kind of musical spontaneity might just overload the pill-addled, pacifier-riddled waste around me, just keep it steady, straight and thorough, four to the floor, whip these constant beats down this corridor of escape, slap us into this sonic womb where the bass is so maternal) BOOM-BOOM-BOOM and we submit to the barrage.

WITNESS THE AMAZING ANTI-SOCIAL ASSHOLE WHO BITCHES ENDLESSLY ABOUT THE NATURE OF HIS PEERS WHEN HE SHOULD JUST SHUT THE HELL UP OR GO SOMEWHERE ELSE!

Yeah, where is this bullshit cynicism coming from? This used to be fun, right? I ought to head for the chill room, find my girl, do something.

I'm going to need another

2 deep

`[dextromethorphan/pma/pseudoephedrine/ guafenisin sulfate]`

and I've found Mary talking to some guy who's like twice as big as me with a neck like a Goddamn telephone pole, who also happens to be dressed like an Abercrombie frat boy and I want to just pop him, but like I mentioned, the girth is in his corner, and I'm two pills into my evening, just waiting, hands gripping the wheel at the front of my cerebral cortex, ready for that ZOOM, BAM, BOOM, BADDA-BING kick off, the moment where my veins all fill up with sex and my eyes close over and do that

squiggle squiggle squiggle flutter leftright leftright leftright

tremble/vibration shit that makes the world look like a perfume commercial, all soft and filtered and essentially perfect, but the pills have me agitated more than anything, so I grab her arm and spit,

"C'mon, Mary!"

"Oh, hey, Steve, hey, oh hey" and the eye contact from her is guilty for a split second, like maybe she was *too* interested in what this frat boy had to say, and then she turns it on, the fucking beams, all green iris and dark pupil and long eyelashes and pouting lips and that smile like whiplash and I cave in, all the aggression gone (have my pills just kicked in?) and I'm kind of okay so,

"Who's your friend?"

"Oh, this is Dane. He's very sweet, he's a good soul."

Her pills have already kicked in. Once she's whacked everyone is "sweet."

I picture it, sort of mad again, and she's saying to me, "Honey, this is John Wayne…what was you last name?" "Gacey." from the clown's blood red lips. "Oh yes," she sighs softly, "John Wayne Gacey. He's oh so very sweet, a real gentle creature."

Being innocent and naive and high all the time is about as safe as jogging next to the Grand Canyon with a blindfold on.

And people throwing rocks at you.

And strong winds pervading.

I say a little prayer for her every time we come to these "parties."

"Nice to meet you, Dane. Mary and I have some very important business to attend to somewhere else in the warehouse. Peace."

I grab her arm to pull her away and ask her why she's fucking with me, but there's instant resistance and Dane is puffing his chest out. I let the hand slide and turn away.

Bitches.

I need another

3 deep

`[hydrobromide/dextromethorphan/baking soda/methylcloroisothiazolinone/mdma]`

...and I'm thinking, "Only at a party this wack, shitty, played out, etc. would I ever have to buy a dirty looking disco biscuit pill of specious content from some Ketamine-soaked, half-assed drug middleman who has no idea personally what's inside the pill that he just charged me twenty bucks for. He also apparently has no grasp on the fact that wearing glow-in-the-dark jewelry, a surgical mask, and a Scooby Doo backpack will never, ever, ever look cool, no matter how many drugs are ingested by the collective party consciousness."

HEY, OLD SPORT! MAYBE THIS GUY DOESN'T CARE ABOUT LOOKING COOL! MAYBE, JUST MAYBE, THIS GUY HAS A WAY FUCKED UP HOMELIFE WHERE POPS IS BASHING HIM ALL OVER THE HOUSE WHILE MOMS IS OFF SCREWING THE ROTO-ROOTER MAN, AND ALL HE DOES DURING THE WEEK IS TRY TO LAY LOW, HEAL, AND HIDE! MAYBE THIS "BULLSHIT" IS HIS ONE WAY OF ESCAPE, HIS TINY, GLITTER SOAKED RELEASE THAT HE VISITS FOR JUST A COUPLE OF HOURS EVERY WEEKEND BEFORE HEADING BACK TO HIS VARIATION ON THE DOMESTIC NIGHTMARE! MAYBE THIS MUSIC, AND THESE DRUGS, AND HIS WEEKEND COSTUME, AND HIS WEEKEND PERSONALITY KEEP HIM FROM TAKING HIMSELF OUT HEMINGWAY GUTBLAST STYLE!

Yeah, yeah. Bored with it. My conscience. Hasn't said anything in my favor for a long time.

Where the hell did Mary go? I look back to where she was chatting it up with Dane the Suburban Neanderthal and spot nothing but empty carpet-space.

It's four in the ay em, I've eaten sixty dollars worth of ecstasy, and I can't find my girlfriend.

Fucked.

Quiet for a moment, thinking about loyalty until I realize that I'm three BOOM-BOOM pills BOOM down and the music the Music THE MUSIC(!) is sounding so good I just want to sink it into the base of my fucking skull and vibrate with it like that sequence in that one cartoon (the one with the replicating brooms) where all those strands of color start dancing around with the sonic waves, the red and the green and the blue all shimmering and smashing into each other and they like BOOM what the... oh ... oooooh *leftright leftright squiggle squiggle leftright* BOOM oh SHIT! and my one way flight to Highsville just blasted off at 747 speed so my brain is burning electric and all I can do is listen and dance, pounding feet, pumping heart, and it's all so good, sososodamnright

just dance just dance just dance faster
yes, this feels right just dance the music is G.O.D. here
just
keep
moving
heart beat BOOM-BOOM please don't stop
it's all fucking all of this is fucking
BOOM overandover BOOM-BOOM-BOOM
high
don't stop yes, so (finally) keep dancing

replace my heart with a twelve inch polyurethane cone and turn up the bass just BOOM-BOOM-BOOM-BOOM-BOOM overandover

head nodding, self approval and sweat dripping
burning.
just dancejustdancejustdancedancedancedancedance

HEY, ISN'T YOUR HEART BEATING A LITTLE FAST!? MAYBE YOU SHOULD RELAX, GET SOME WATER! DO YOU FEEL OKAY? WHAT WAS IN THOSE PILLS? WHERE'S YOUR GIRLFRIEND? WHAT'S YOUR GIRLFRIEND'S NAME? WHERE'S DANE? WHAT ARE THEY

DOING? WHAT DID YOU EAT TONIGHT?

...fucking conscience.

BOOM this is all too good, I don't feel like thinking about myself ANYMORE! (I don't feel like thinking).

Escape.

Where's that kid in the surgical mask, he's my brother now and

I need another

4 deep

[dextromethorphan]

What a riot, buying a pill from a fourteen year old girl wearing tin foil angel wings. Looked a bit like my little sister so I felt guilty for wanting to run my tongue down the crack of her ass.

YOU ARE LOW CLASS AND LOST, MY FRIEND! PLEASE GET SOME WATER! JUST ONE BOTTLE OF WATER AND I'LL BE QUIET! YOU ARE COOKING YOUR BRAIN! DON'T PUSH IT!

Oh, wait, don't move for a second and let my eyes re-orient themselves, I can't see straight and it's *leftright leftright leftright leftright leftright leftright leftright leftright leftright leftright* it won't stop now, I can't focus *leftright leftright leftright*

leftright leftright leftright leftright leftright leftright leftright leftright.

I want to dance/I can't even see. No match up. Dysfunction. Lacking the proper means.

SUNBURST behind my eyes, FLASH like a punch to the skull, only it came from *inside* my head, and I want to throw up.

WHERE THE HELL IS MARY?

I have to sit down (I feel five years old right now and I'm scared and I'm shaking).

So *hot*, just curl up, maybe someone will bring me water, I'm sweating so hard, I can feel it pooling at my lower back, dripping from my armpits, and I have to close up (pill bug, HA) and shut down for a little bit, and I close my eyes and thousands of crystal castles are being built and destroyed on the inside of my eyelids but it's not comforting or beautiful, it's not real at all, it's not the reason I came here (right?) and now I'm not dancing and *there's Mary* standing ten feet away and she doesn't see me and she's not alone and oh my God there's that frat boy and he's got his hand on her ass and she's kissing his neck like she used to kiss mine and I can't see where her hands are but one of her elbows is moving with a steady rhythm that breaks my heart and aren't they both so Goddamned sweet and healthy and why isn't she looking for me I'm right over here on the floor and there's another SUNBURST and my head, my head, my head oh

oh

oh

fuck

oh God forgive me.

I want to rest now.

{shutdown, stasis, near myocardial failure, distension of vessels proximal to the brain, fluctuating consciousness, regurgitation}

I HATE TO COME OFF AS A SELF-RIGHTEOUS CONSCIENCE HERE PAL, BUT YOU'VE NEARLY KILLED US TONIGHT SO I FEEL JUSTIFIED WHEN I SAY,

"I TOLD YOU SO!"

shut up

Eight ay em in the morning.

Lonely, biologically toxic, near dead.

Smiling because I just found an accidentally discarded pill on the floor.

I open my mouth, close my mouth, swallow my poison escape route.

I step into the morning sun and pray that I burn today and shed these corrupted cells, this weak shell.

From the ashes, the million tiny phoenixes of my flesh,

pure and skybound.

Ascendance

This last place bothers me. Everything breaks down when you go inside.

Even you. You will collapse, but you'll see the rest of what you've been looking for. There are no explanations in there. Only an unfolding.

No pain, but no real joy either. It's almost nothing.

But it's a better kind of nothing than I could show you in the lower circles.

There's a weird hum to the place that makes my ears feel like they're bleeding even though they are not.

Whatever you thought you knew, it'll melt down in there.

It'll liquefy and start humming. Vibrating. There's a sequence to it I can't peg, a rhythm under the buzz.

Listen to it, and maybe for once, the world will make sense.

Maybe, if you listen close, things will add up.

Maybe there's an answer in there.

What's that? Oh, "What's the question?" Well, not to go Zen on you here, but what *isn't* the question?

Clean the blood off your hands before you go.

III. TRANCE END/A Number of Things Come to Mind

The Clearing At the End

4 Morning of August 23, 2002, 7:06am

When Quincy woke on the twenty-third of August in Our Year of the Lord 2002, his mind had been overcome with numbers. All he could think was one, two, three, over and over again. Those three numbers, the first we learn, the first things drawn in chalk after A, B, and C, were all Quincy had left in his mind, repeating in an endless loop, a mathematic mantra stuck in the skipping record of Quincy's gray matter. Quincy could not find a reason, or the will, or even the physical control to rise from his bed and greet the day. Quincy's mind had become the VCR that God never bothered to read the instructions to, flashing over and over in the dark. One, two, three, one, two, three, one, two, three, one, two, three, one, two, three...

The Path...

1 Morning of August 22, 2002, 12:31pm

12:31 will work. 12:32 will work. 12:33 has a Trinity in it, as in two plus one is three, and within the rules these two can be added since they are separated by the colon, and then the produced three is placed next to the two additional threes forming the digital Father, Son, and Holy Ghost. God in the numbers. You feel kind of pure if you rise when the alarm clock reads 12:33, like maybe if you let the Trinity into your head God won't fuck you up so bad this particular day. Good odds.

12:34 though, that's the winner. Sequential, one plus two is three, one plus three is four, and their reversals, and the whole batch adds up to ten, as in base ten, the foundation of our system, which put all these numbers in my brain in the first place. 12:34 is classic. Absolutely classic.

I watch the little digital figures realign, then 12:34, in all its perfection, is right there in my face, and I've got 60 seconds to roll myself out of bed before the less than ideal 12:35 clicks on and ruins my day.

I'm trapped in the shower for 48 minutes until 1:23 hits, allowing my exit. I occupy the time by memorizing shampoo ingredients (methylchlorisothiazolinone is a favorite, it's all prefix and has the same number of letters as the alphabet) and counting the holes in the shower head as the steam turns me pruny and leaves red streaks where the water courses down my shoulders, back, ass, and legs.

I stayed at my friend Chris' apartment two months ago and got "stuck" in the shower. I counted tiles for close to an hour, until his hot water became so frigid it sucked my breath down the drain with it. I emerged dead white and when he asked what took me so long the first thing that came to mind to respond with was, "Masturbation. I was masturbating. It was great!"

Keeping an obsession secret means "engaging in subterfuge." I prefer calling it that. Lying is haggard.

Lying is fucking necessary. Lying is the oil that keeps my duplicitous little lifestyle from overheating and turning into a grand and messy debacle. When you're an obsessive-compulsive, pill popping raver who works forty hours a week as a commercial loan analyst for a very reputable company, lying becomes your life's blood. I'd dry up and die without it, i.e.:

Do they have the credit to support that kind of debt?

Absolutely.

Are these e-bombs clean?

Clean as rocky mountain waters, man.

So you'd recommend I avoid the annuities in favor of increased debt?

Ultimately, in this kind of tumultuous financial atmosphere, this kind of loan is the only sure thing. So yes, and I'm telling you this as a favor.

What'd you think of my set, dude?

Best fucking psy-trance, deep house, gay French happy hardcore combo I've ever heard. Fucking royal, man. Plus you got the chicks fucking dripping for you. The best. A-number-fucking-1 brilliant man!

The debt to income ratio seems a little rough. Can they afford this loan?

You have to look at the context on this one. Trust me, pigmy goats will outsell even the Bavarian grass-seed this year. It's a boom market.

Tell me it's not the pills. Will you tell me you really love me, baby?

Butterfly Jasmine Moonbeam, you are the most radiant, genuine, beautiful person I've ever met, and for me not to love you would be like asking God to reach down and pull my soul out and stomp it into a hundred ugly pieces. Of course I love you. Of course. Of course, of course, Oh God, OF COURSE! It's impossible not to love you, you have so much energy, and even though we've just met tonight, I know that for us to not share this energy would be a tragedy, and I'd regret it forever. In fact, I need to be closer to your energy right now.

What took you so long in the shower?

I was masturbating. It was great!

Lies are the shortest way to reach one's goals, fulfill needs. I'm not devious, just efficient.

Psychopath is a label.

My late afternoon breakfast is Cocoa Crunch. I eat 88 inflated sugar puffs, eight per spoonful, eleven bites total. 88 works for me, and although I love the balance of the figure I always feel an unnecessary guilt in regards to the whole associative Nazi thing. The eighth letter of the alphabet is H. 88=HH. 88=Heil Hitler. My cereal consumption has no sublimated Hitler love in its pattern. 88 puffs fills me up. That's it.

The proper time rolls over on my watch and I'm out the door with my car keys jangling.

2 Afternoon of August 22, 2002, 2:34pm

As Quincy drove across the South Belton Bypass on his way to work his mind clouded over and familiarity navigated. His subconscious was at the steering wheel, his autonomic system was regulating each breath and beat, his conscious mind was barely registering the passage of time and space. Every day, five days a week, he spent an average of fourteen minutes on the road to work, barring unforeseen circumstances like auto wrecks, construction, or the sudden metamorphosis of the pavement into a raging, great-white-shark-filled ocean. This last circumstance was unlikely, but Quincy harbored the irrational fear that the world could someday suddenly turn to liquid beneath him. In this liquid he knew *they* were waiting for him, the sharks, the great beasts, swimming in circles, staring black-eyed soulless stares at the surface, hungry, razor-sharp, and ready to consume him.

Solid pavement rushes underneath Quincy's car as he zones out to a near meditation level on the Bypass. The thirty two beat/four measure syncopation of Jungle music blasting from his speakers pulls his brain into a level of sedate stasis. The density of the sound, the constant nature of the beats, over and over and over again with very little change barring the occasional machine breakdown noise, all of this feels *right* to Quincy's brain. It matches his thought patterns, frantic and repetitious at the same time. One hundred and sixty beats per minute is Quincy's preferred tempo. Quincy has, on five separate occasions, had his heart beating at the exact same tempo for periods of time long enough to exhaust most hummingbirds. The third time this occurred Quincy suffered a severe case of "ratchet jaw" and nearly ground his teeth away. He could taste the enamel chips and tiny shreds of old fillings as he noshed away his face. As Quincy ground his teeth to the smoothness of river rock his brain was stuck repeating the alliteration, "Many milligrams of meth, many milligrams of meth..." The shady e-bombs he bought often contained more meth than trailer park ground water.

Quincy wakes up from his drive-induced stupor just in time to park his Hyundai very attentively between the two faded yellow lines that indicate his spot at Sycorp Financing. Quincy loves the symmetry of a good parking job.

The next three hours find Quincy going through his motions. He processes, annotates, inquires, faxes, copies, designates, allocates, designs, aligns, contacts, files, piles, and manipulates. He twists numbers that illustrate weak income until they represent a sterling borrowing base. He smiles at co-workers and laughs at jokes without really listening to them. Quincy is not at work to interact. He is here because he loves numbers, and stability, and patterns, and dependability. He loves acronyms and tries to construct sentences out of them, which phonetically sound like gibberish. *We're gonna have to hepmar the roa if we don't want a deeker off the admin pee icey, right?*

As the right side of Quincy's brain tabulates fourteen months of collected gross income adjusted in relation to five years of projected annual overhead, the left side of Quincy's brain blackens. The blackness spreads in his mind, nulling and voiding what were once creative synaptic spaces, bits of colorful gray matter that lived outside of patterns and contained beauty and inspiration. The blackness spreads rapidly, like an ignited charcoal snake. The right side of Quincy's brain, where Quincy's soul had recently taken up residence in order to avoid the logicancer that ravished the left lobe, could not care less about the loss of the creative forces.

"Fuck it," Quincy thought rationally, "I've got a 401k."

"I've got my numbers," Quincy thought, and the part of his character that still resided in the atrophied wasteland of his creative mind caused him to break out in goosebumps.

After working a tiny bit of overtime Quincy gets ready to head home, already anticipating the ordered chaos of the night's rave in nearby Salem. As the clock clicks over to

6:23pm (reverse multipliers always work for Quincy) the automatic doors that open onto Sycorp Financing's foyer close behind him, and he's headed home.

3 Evening of August 22, 2002 11:11pm

Rats live on no evil star.

Picture, then, the virtuous star, swarming with vermin. Like this place. This fucking place is hip deep in vermin of homo sapiens appearance. The reverse palindromic logic plays out.

RADAR is the name of this party. Right now every element of the evening is soaked in palindromes, the time, the date, even the damn year, which is rare. I haven't been this excited about a year since 1991.

I arrived at the warehouse at 10:11 (a beautiful spoken sequential) and was greeted by the familiar sight of speaker towers, sacramentally lit DJ booths, and hundreds of bodies moving in mathematically precise patterns.

It's always the same at these raves, the same bodies, stuck in the same motions, the same minds locked into the same patterns of urge and abuse. It's just like my work, all process, no progress. We move in these patterns, we manipulate them, but we never force the answers out of them. I'm looking for something in the patterns, during my more hopeful moments. I'd say data catharsis, but that's not quite right.

Digital cleansing is closer.

When the acid hits me quick like this the connection speed goes way up. The Lucy I bought from Mortis the

Tortoise is racing through my brain like a power line dropped in a bucket of salt water.

A boy who appears to be about fifteen is standing to the right of me. He is nodding his head mechanically and holding his left hand over his heart. His right hand is stiff, fingers outstretched, and as he shuffles his feet with the music his hand traces the form of the cross from his head to his belly and then shoulder to shoulder. The Catholic raver is easy to spot. They swallow their MDMA communion and then wash over with guilt and serotonin at the same time. Thus, the rhythmic supplication.

The girl in the baby blue tank top to my left has made the same figure eight motion with her arms over two hundred times.

I'm not the only one stuck in these patterns. I'm aware of it, that's the difference.

I'm dancing listlessly to some boring four/four tech house, trying to get my brain deeper into its patterns, but it seems to be too simple. It's just one, two, three, four, one, two, three, four, over and over again, the least inventive drum pattern on Earth.

Bored. Four hits of acid deep and I'm bored.

I'm watching a golden frog make love to a gorgeous Aboriginal woman with purple eyes. This is happening on my left shoe. It's a worthless, meaning free visual, and I'm bored with it. This tech house is intolerable and the inevitable stink of rave sweat is bringing my dinner back up my throat for a second appearance.

Time to up the ante and try it. Time to give in to the temptation that always hits me at these parties. Time to exercise my affinity for all things Trinity, the big 3 x 3, tres squared, nine hits of liquid. Three threes, nine at once. If I can ingest nine hits of acid at one time, the Father, Son, and Holy Ghost will all jump behind my eyes and show me some pulsing, blinding, "tear it all down and restructure the fiber of reality in a new and superior way" type glory. The numbers work. Nothing beats the Trinity.

I've got the money for it. I do the footwork and spot my target, who appears to be selling some ecstasy to a family of four, two teens, a nervous dad, and a soccer mom.

Some say the rave scene has gone mainstream.

I wait for the Bradys to bail with their dope and then I make my transaction. Thirty dollars in Mortis the Tortoise's pocket later I've got a carefully dropped puddle of liquid Lucy in the palm of my left hand. Mortis thought I was crazy, but he's ultimately a capitalist, and has a hard time placing ethics or the safety of others above profit. So, he's got enough money to buy a couple of CD's and I've got enough acid to fry a herd of elephants.

I hesitate for twenty two seconds, pulse slamming with fear, the kind easily overcome by desire. Then I drop my face to my palm and quickly lap up my path to righteous digital cleansing.

3 x 3. A perfect triangle consuming my mind.

As if my act of faith had been rewarded the music slamming into us from the speakers speeds up and increases in density. The beats get faster and faster, grow closer and closer together, until they seem like dots forming a straight line of sound. I rush up to the front right speaker bank, and just as I get within two feet of the bass cones the interminable build crashes like a wave and a breakbeat almost knocks the air out of me. These piston driven speakers force the beats into my bones and vibrate my connective tissue. The sound is so thick here. I'm on the edge of a roaring forest fire, and for a moment I smell smoke. Then cotton candy, and I'm smelling it with every pore on my face, sucking in the smell through a million tiny mouths on the surface of my flesh.

"Oh fucking shit! Yeaaah!!!" someone screams to the right of me. My thoughts exactly. Jungle makes me feel like that, it contains ecstatic patterns, vortexes and sound-whorls. Being this close to the speakers gives me the sensation of being tossed around by a sonic tornado. The decibels are giving the mathematic and relentless jungle music substance, flesh. It is here to deliver us.

I stand erect in front of the speakers with my palms facing towards the sound, subject to it.

I close my eyes, and for one second I recognize the madness (123) of what I've done. There are thirteen total hits of acid doing God knows what in my brain right now. I have done this in pursuit of a vision, an escape. Part of me wants to run to the hospital right now and hook up a thorazine drip before this chemical roller coaster hits the drop.

I ingested the Trinity. It is too late.

I can feel the air from the bass impact cooling me in my ocean of acid-sweat, vibrating every tiny hair on my body. In my head it sounds like a high pitch whine is being run through a vocoder, getting louder and louder...

eeeee...eeeeeeeeeee...eeeeeeeeeeeeeee...eeeeeeeeeeeeeee eeeeeeeeeeeeeeee...

Then the doses hit at once and the world blurs thick in front of me like clear wax had just been poured into my eyes and when it washes away there are three trees in front of me dropping fruit and the fruit itself is made of crystals, millions of tiny, precise, and exact crystals, and I see people with no legs dragging themselves up to the trees and trying to bite into the fruit, which then whirls at blurring speed and shreds their faces into mists of bone and

"Oh shit! This dude's eyes are rolling back in his head. Dude, are..."

blood, and the blood gets pulled into the soil by these tiny blue veins that twitch like surfacing worms and grow thick with the blood of the legless people, whose bodies are decomposing into soft puddles, which are

"Rachel just ignore that. Some loady always has to fuck up the vibe, huh?"

themselves absorbed into the roots of the tree, and I look up from the ground and see these armless people walking in perfect circles around the tree, bellowing these low, threnodic moans, and some of them are staring at me, their eyes emptied of hope, and I'm trying to make sense of this when suddenly I'm looking at my hands, and they are moving without control, each

"Just fucking back up here, people! He needs air. Somebody get the EMT..."

of them in front of me, tracing patterns that emit sound, like crystal humming, and I realize my hands are chasing each other along the infinite path of a Mobius Strip, and I feel something opening up in my head, and then I'm falling backwards and when I land and regain my footing I am

"..repeat, we are in transit to Mercy Central, we should arrive within..."

looking at two identical versions of myself, there are three of me in this small, black room, and I am inside each of us, all three of me (123), and we are pushing small wooden pegs into our hands, through the tissue, which welts around the wooden pegs until the surface can't bear the tension, and the peg pushes into our burst hands and numbers swirl out of the hole and rush up my arm and the numbers (123), millions of them, a vast legion of crawling

"...we need a chemstat CPC, and intubate him if he continues to..."

numbers are seething over our/my skin, eating away at it, chewing down to the bones, chewing in through my eyes to my brain, where they begin to circle, trapped, storming and then all I can see is a huge, dark orange sky

"Please restrain his arms, Peters, he could seriously harm himself if..."

swimming in numbers (123), and the pattern formed by the endless millions is pushing directly into me, into I, into my eye, which is perfect because eye is the name of the Trinity, Zeyeon, Eyesis, Oseyeris, I and Eye, three letters, each with three extensions when printed EYE, that perfect three at the center

"That's not possible. How can there be no brain signal at all? He's breathing."

of it all, every element of my existence has always been here in my mind, there is nowhere else worth being but here, God and eye are one, three in one, three in 1, 3 in 1, 3,2,1,1,1,1,...

1,2,3,1,2,3,1,2,3,1,2,3,

1,

2,

3

1

These numbers are all I ever needed. It is all I am. I am One. Two. Three.

The Witness At Dawn

Dale believed in both Christ and karma. But no matter how many prayers fell desperate from his lips, or how often he reminded himself of the reparations he'd made, he couldn't shake the guilt. It seethed through him, the heat-wired electricity of niacin flush. It wracked his stomach, left him with cramps that ran the length of his twisting guts.

Whoever killed Mark, Pete, and Steve, they're coming for me next.

The pistol was new to Dale, heavy and alien to his touch. Never had much affinity for guns. Tried to run his life quiet, calm. Tried to be a peaceful person.

That's why New Orleans never should have happened.

But it did, and now his friend's houses were sectioned off by yellow police tape, and he was cowering around his cold apartment clutching an oily gun.

Cops had asked Dale questions he couldn't answer.

"Do you know if your friends were involved in any sort of cult?"

"Maybe something to do with rituals?"

"Can you think of anyone who would want them dead?"

This last question was accompanied by long, sunlamp stares.

They think I did this. Want me to crack. But I *didn't do anything.*

And Dale couldn't help feeling that his friends got their just desserts. Not an easy thought, but it felt true.

He'd hid the news clipping in a cupboard three days ago, after getting the call about Pete's death. But Dale knew the picture was there. Meghan Farrington, her face newsprint gray, smiling from the obituary page. Twenty-eight years old.

She was twenty-seven when we met her in New Orleans. Told us charming stories about her father, Earl, a "Nawlins gris-gris man" who supposedly sold fake mojo to tourists and real hoodoo to locals.

She wasn't looking when Mark slipped the roofie in her bourbon. He promised we wouldn't hurt her; said she wouldn't even remember. But how could she not remember them? Pushing her down. Taking their turns. Steve, rotten on tequila, calling her by his ex's name, punching her kidneys. How could she not remember, with those bruises?

But I didn't do anything. I just held the camera and filmed them and pretended to laugh while they played with their rag-doll. I'm not like them. Never touched her.

And afterwards, when that evening's ugliness had cancer-crawled its way through the men's friendship and set them adrift from each other, Dale had tried to set things right.

He'd seen Meghan's driver's license that night and knew her name. Took him less than a day to find her on the internet.

Dale forged a friendship with her, posing online as a woman named Susan Jessup. He learned how fragile Meghan had become. That night at Mardi Gras now kept the girl isolated, house-bound.

Trust had become impossible, but somehow she'd opened up to "Susan Jessup," who claimed to have been a victim of similar abuse.

Dale felt crooked as hell, but couldn't let himself abandon Meghan after he'd helped to bring her to this state. He could fix things...

And when she revealed that she was pregnant, Dale mailed her cash. He skimped on his own groceries, settling for ramen every night so he could mail Meghan money for the child his old friends had raped into her.

Even these things didn't assuage Dale's guilt.

He burned the New Orleans tape; took it to the landfill and blazed it to lighter-fluid vapors. Green-black smoke in the moonlight. Dale prayed to Christ that what had been done might be undone, might be smashed to ashes like the burning tape.

But now Meghan was dead. Her un-named child had passed with her. Dale had been scanning the Announcements page, expecting news of Meghan's baby, when he saw her picture looking out from the opposing section.

"Complications during delivery." God, obituaries were always so sanitary. She and the child had been dead four days, their murderers hidden nine months back behind a rohypnol haze.

And those murderers were dead now, too. The karmic ocean had pulled them down to darker currents.

But I tried to make things right. Whoever killed my friends has to know that.

Dale dead-bolted the front door and slid the chain-latch into place. Whoever was coming would have to get past that first. He'd have them at gunpoint.

He settled into his bed, pistol on the night-stand with the safety switched off, sheets soaking up sweat.

3:14AM. No one knocking on his door. Maybe he had set things right. Maybe whoever was seeking revenge for Meghan knew that Dale wasn't like the others. Maybe...

"Dale..."

A woman's whisper.

A shape at the foot of the bed.

It was her. Hospital robe wet against her skin, stained dark. Arms cradling a child, tiny, still trailing its umbilical.

She moved quickly, skittering on slightly bowed legs to the right edge of his bed, where Dale lay paralyzed, his gun an abstraction of metal he'd never understood.

"Hold your child, Dale."

She laid the newborn on his chest. Its head lifted, wide new eyes staring into Dale's. The New Orleans video footage was playing on a frantic loop in its all-black pupils. And the child began to cry, the wail of something lost knowing it won't find home.

Dale looked to Meghan's eyes, pleading.

"But, please, Meghan... I didn't do anything!"

"No. You didn't."

The infant's hands reached up, covering Dale's sight. They smelled heavily of gun oil. Tiny fingers curled in like talons and began to pull with the strength of a grown man's hands.

And as Dale felt his eyes being torn loose he knew that something terrible had been done and was, at last, being undone.

Cortical Reorganization

Mandy Vasquez let the sun soak in, hoping to retain the day's heat when cold, wet night rolled in and left her shaking. She'd begged up enough cash to score tonight, so at least there was one guaranteed warm evening ahead of her.

"Listen, lady, do you want some money or not?"

"Oh, sorry..." Mandy hobbled over to the blue sedan, maintaining a delicate balance on mismatched prosthetic feet (the left—a curved spring meant for disabled athletes, the right—a regular foot with fake skin that swelled on rainy nights). She snatched the cash from the woman's hand, caught the smell of a new perm.

Gotta stop zoning. I'd be out three bucks if that light would have turned green.

Mandy stepped back to the curb thinking this new intersection was working out fine. She'd only been in Portland for a few days, but they seemed pretty free with the cash. She made sure her sign—DISABLED, WAITING ON SSI, PLEASE HELP GOD BLESS!—was upright, then flinched as a streak of pain ran through the sole of her non-existent right foot.

That was the worst, the terrible pain in feet she didn't even have. Like being forced to give birth to a kid you weren't allowed to keep. Hurting for nothing at all.

That's why she got high—it killed the ugly feeling that ripped through her missing heels, like hooks driven through meat, tugging ever upwards. The dope let that agony sluice into the gutters and trickle to nothing.

Another shock of pain hit the space where she didn't exist. She held back tears and lifted her sign higher.

Martin Vasquez hated the drive home. Early summer weather had him cooking. Run the A/C—kill the ozone. Open the windows—fill your lungs with exhaust. No conscionable way to avoid roasting.

Today was worse. March 14th. Mandy's birthday.

She's thirty-one today, if she's still alive.

March 14th meant pounding booze and pretending the wreck never happened. Pretending that he'd stayed awake, that he'd buckled Mandy in. Wishing he and Estrella hadn't been so young and poor when Mandy needed them to be rich and mature and strong. Wishing that he had it all to do again, to never abandon his crippled four-year-old in the fruit section of a Shop-Rite.

Mandy had such beautiful brown eyes, with flecks of gold in them. He still saw them, some nights. Stupid dreams.

He rounded 13th and his fresh-bought bottle of SoCo rustled in its paper sack.

You talkin' to me, buddy? Let's get started.

Martin twisted the cap loose, let it click to the plastic floor-mat beneath his feet. Quick cop-scan, then he knocked back two stern slugs, let the burn spread.

He pictured the calendar in his kitchen, today's date reading "Mandy 31." Easier to swallow another shot, let his focus go soft.

Martin pulled up to a four way intersection and spotted movement to his right.

Mandy wished the man would let go of her hand. The light would go green soon, people would start honking. This guy was interrupting the flow of her grind.

"I've seen your eyes in my dreams," he said.

"That's dreams for you. Now let go of my hand and get the hell out of here."

You had to be stern with the freaks.

The man flinched at her words, shook his head.

"Yeah...sorry..." He dropped his gaze to the bottle in his lap. Mandy pulled away quickly, happy she still held the twenty he'd waved at her.

The light turned green and after a moment's pause, the man drove on.

Mandy hardly noticed. She was thinking of tonight's score and the liquid pleasure that would roll through her limbs and calm the screaming phantoms haunting the places where she'd died.

The Seat of Reason

It wasn't that they really wanted the fucking fish. Mary just wanted Sofie to stop crying.

Sofie was only eight but she'd been a trooper through the bankruptcy, and the move, and adjusting to her new school. She hadn't even fussed when Michael got the Ryerson Corp job, even though it meant her dad would be spending half of every month in China. But after that the days were too long. Portland winter crept in. Mary spent more and more on wine so she could sleep at night. Sofie withdrew, and pined for her dad's return.

And Mary felt the girl needed—deserved—so much. Instead she got the Abbot family shit-show, which now included a full blown fight, Mary and Michael raging at each other in the kitchen the night before.

So when Mary woke to the sound of Sofie crying she knew the girl had heard their fight and she rushed in, desperate to make things right. She remembered the one gift that had been on Sofie's wish list through the last two Christmases and decided that if Sofie couldn't have stability, or her dad, or a mom who was always the bright, shining light she wanted to be then she could, at the very least, have those goddamn fish.

It was quiet on the drive to the pet store, Michael saying nothing, his face expressionless the way it got when he decided a fight wasn't over. Mary ignored it, focused on Sofie.

"What kind of fish do you like?"

"The ones with the sideway eyes. Or the rainbow ones where you can see their hearts."

"Well, I'm not sure on that first one, but I think we can find you some very colorful fish."

"And a pirate ship? With bubbles?"

"Sure."

"And a robot named Food-tron that feeds them?"

"Um..."

"And a YouTube show where I talk to the fish and they use a special microphone to talk back?"

Mary caught Michael smiling. This was a game Sofie played, asking ever more ridiculous questions until he broke out laughing.

"And a shrink-a-tizer and scuba suit so I can go in and ride the fish?"

Sofie paused, eyeing Michael, calculating.

"How about some robot arms for the fish, so we can play volleyball with a piece of cereal and then I can get high fives?"

Michael lost it, and laughed. Sofie laughed with him, and the sight of that was enough to bring a smile to Mary's face.

Sofie chose neon tetras, their bright blue and red stripes glowing in the tank lights. The flesh above their stripes was translucent in a way which made Mary uncomfortable. It felt strange to see inside living things.

When she was six her brother Trevor wrecked his BMX in their family's cul-de-sac. She heard the crunch before she saw the compound fracture, his collarbone jutting red-white. After Sofie was born Mary had baby-proofed their house until it was a maze of gates and padding. She wanted to do the same to their new place, but Sofie was eight. Michael would tell her it was absurd. Still, she cringed whenever Sofie stumbled toward the stone hearth of their fireplace or the glass edges of their dinner table.

A pet store employee noticed them browsing. "What can I get you folks?"

Mary looked to Sofie. "You want to tell him?"

"Uh-huh. These guys." She pointed to the tetras. "Ten of 'em."

The employee glanced at the tank in their cart. "To make it healthy, you want about one living thing per gallon. Would you like to start with four, and make sure they're happy before you add more?"

Sofie nodded. "If I can have five then I want that frog."

"Well, let me talk to mom and dad about that real quick."

The employee turned to Mary and Michael.

"I can sell you one of those frogs, but sometimes they eat the fish. Or the fish eat them and swim around with a leg hanging out of their mouth. One time I found a frog trying to mate with a dead fish, so…it'd be a lot to explain to a kid."

Michael said, "Just the fish for now."

"Awww. Come on." An edge crept into Sofie's voice.

Please don't let this go bad.

Sofie scanned the tank. Her eyes brightened. "How about one of these guys?" She pointed to a tiny snail with a dark black shell sliding its way up the tank.

Mary pictured herself saying no to the snail, standing there with Sofie growing sullen and Michael getting frustrated.

No. We deserve a good day.

So they drove home with four neon tetras and one snail in a plastic bag full of chemically-treated tank water.

The thing they didn't understand was how one snail could make so many more. Within weeks you could barely see the fish unless you focused your eyes past the hundreds of tiny new snails.

Michael yelled to Mary from the office. "Wiki says a lot of these guys aren't only guys, like they have both parts. It says 'ovotestes.' They have tubes and glands so they can secrete eggs and sperm into different pockets in their body and just knock themselves up."

Sofie looked worried. "The man at the pet store said only five creatures in the tank. Are my fish going to get sick?"

Mary pictured the snails swarming the fish at night, seething in through their gills.

"No. They'll be okay. Dad's going to clean out the snails."

"Promise? They bother me at night. They move around the whole time and their shadows crawl on the walls."

"Promise."

Mary woke the next morning to find Michael at the dinner table, hunched over an emptied aquarium. The tetras were in the kitchen, circling in a Pyrex measuring cup. The dining room stank, seaweed rotting at the shore.

"I think I got them all." Michael gestured to the graveyard of smashed snails on the table, fragmented shells and shiny black ichor spotting the paper towels he'd used to swipe the infestation from the tank.

"You up all night?"

"Yeah. Wanted to be sure this was done before I took off for work."

"Shit. That's today? Already?"

Something moved on the table. Michael wrapped his finger in a fresh paper towel and used it to crush the escaping snail.

He looked at Mary. The circles under his eyes had never been darker. He looked beyond her to the clock on the stove.

"I need a shower more than anything else. I'm barely going to make my plane. Any chance you can—"

"I've got this. Just go."

She wasn't really sure she was telling the truth. She looked over the tiny dead things on her kitchen table and wanted to set the whole thing on fire.

Do I have this?

And then Michael was gone, and she had no choice but to keep going, and the air was heavy around her even before Sofie woke up screaming.

Mary had grown up with migraines. At first she figured it was now Sofie's turn on that particularly shitty carousel of pain.

She pressed a cool washcloth to Sofie's forehead. "Is it cloudy in your vision, baby? Like snow passing from one side of your eyes to the other?"

Sofie moaned. "It's so sharp, mom. In the front, by my eyes."

She placed her hand on Sofie's chest. "It'll pass. Trust me, okay? It always passes."

She stayed by the girl's side, sleeping fitfully in the La-Z-Boy in Sofie's reading corner.

The first time something woke her it was a buzzing text notification—Michael had landed at Zhengzhou.

The second time she woke was when Sofie sat straight up in bed.

"Sof?"

The girl said nothing. Mary rose from her chair and put a hand on her daughter's shoulder, and that was when a gush of clear fluid erupted from the girl's nostrils and dripped from her chin to the front of her PJ's.

With that, Sofie flopped back to her pillow and kept sleeping.

The way the girl collapsed alarmed her mother, but Mary'd had snotty migraines before and Sofie's breathing sounded clear after that, so she stripped the messy shirt and returned to her chair.

In the morning Mary noticed thin black rivulets in the crusted mucus on Sofie's shirt, but by then Sofie was up and moving and hungry. She seemed okay. Mary was so relieved that she broke down crying the moment she returned from dropping the girl at school.

Whatever your kid does, that's because of you.

The kid hands an old lady a batch of dandelions at the park, or the teacher says her book report is exceptional, and all of that is a reflection of your good parenting.

But if you accept that, you have to accept this too. You and Michael did this.

Sofie sat on the couch, staring straight ahead.

"Did the girl attack you? Was she bullying you?"

No answer.

"Sofie, you know we're always honest with each other, and you know I'll always love you. But I have to understand what happened. And you're not allowed back at school for a while, so we've got plenty of time to talk. I understand if you need time to process what happened. Violent things are scary for everybody involved."

Sofie turned toward her mother.

"I wasn't scared, mom. Not at all. There was a bad feeling in my head. After I pushed Emma off the monkey bars I felt good again."

Mary dizzied and sat quickly on the couch. She thought of what the principal had said. How they found Sofie staring at Emma and her broken arm, just watching her scream.

Sofie said, "I'm hungry."

Mary looked into Sofie's eyes and saw nothing of her daughter.

"Jesus...do you know what time it is here?"

"You need to come home. Now."

"I'm home in nine days. This is our *only* job right now."

"It's Sofie."

"Fuck. Is she hurt?"

"No...it's...she got in trouble at school, and when I try to talk to her, something is *wrong*."

"I talked to her on the phone last night. She was quiet, but she seemed fine. Probably bummed I'm gone. I promise when I get back we'll have a good weekend together. We'll—"

"She's not fine. You can't see it because you're not here. But I can see it, because I'm the only fucking one here and—"

"Have you been drinking?"

"Fuck you."

And Mary would have hung up then, but worry brought her back to the phone. "The way she's talking, if you look at her when she's doing it...something's off since she had that migraine. It was awful. She got the bad snots like I used to."

"Shit. I know. I'm sorry. And *that* makes sense now."

"What?"

"The night before I left I saw a mess on her pillow. It's crazy—at first I thought it was from those goddamn snails, after I found them in her carpet. She was making these weird little sounds while I was packing, and I went to check on her and the carpet was fucking crunchy with those things. That's why I didn't sleep that night—I didn't want to leave all that mess for you."

"Why didn't you tell me that?"

"I don't know. I didn't want there to be one more stressful, shitty thing between us. And I knew you'd freak out, so I took care of it. But I'm glad you reminded me about the migraine snots. I got so paranoid when I saw her pillow that I felt around her bed checking for snails. Can you believe that?"

"You think there could have been a virus in those things? Like when you stepped on them something got in the air and—"

"Babe, you've got to get some rest, okay? I love you. I'll be there soon, and we'll work through this, and..."

When she realized he wasn't *really* listening, and wasn't coming home, Mary set the phone on the bed and knew she was alone.

Mary imagined a slash on a timeline dividing when Sofie was well and when she became sick, a bright red chasm between their old life and a new world where the girl seemed broken and Mary disappeared and became an engine of repair, aware she existed only when she saw her hollowed-out reflection in the mirror.

Time distorted, each new day an awful version of Sofie's escalating questions game.

"What do you do when your child only smiles if you smile first, and one side of her face hangs slack?"

"And what if she says 'We need more food.' but her belly is already distended and you say, 'We?' and the girl stares ahead and doesn't respond? Do you turn on the TV to make her near-catatonia seem purposeful?"

"And if you wake at some ungodly hour to find your child leaning over your sleeping body, her mouth wide open as if to scream, her face shining beneath the torrent of fluid running from her nose, what part of your mind allows you to simply tuck her back in and wipe her face and pretend it had not happened?"

"And what do you make of the phone call from the pet store the next morning—the voice on the phone saying, 'We've had an unexpected issue with some of our aquatic companions, and we'd love to speak to you in person. There are some cleaning recommendations we'd like to give you, and a release form we need to have signed, so if you're willing to drop by today we'd really appreciate that.'?"

"And what do you tell the pediatrician's office when they ask about the nature of your visit? Do you tell them about the snails, and risk some delusional diagnosis of your own? And when they refer you to a child psychologist do you realize that this will never end?"

"And when the psychiatrist is done with your child and he says, 'The callousness and lack of responsiveness is a real concern, but this could be temporary. I'm not sure we have enough to justify an MRI.' and you think about your long nights on the computer, trying to figure out what's happening, and you ask if it might be psychopathy and the doctor says, 'We're calling it empathy disorder now, because of the stigma. But it's a possibility we can't rule out.' and your daughter wipes another gush of clear fluid from her nose across her filthy sleeve, and you feel the floor open up beneath you—after all that happens do you think you might want to die, just to stop feeling this?"

"And where the hell is Michael? And why won't he answer his phone?"

Mary wondered, later, what might have happened if she had grabbed the bottle of wine on the way *back* from the hospital. But the feverish nightmare of her day had clouded her mind, and she'd forgotten. Besides, Sofie was finally sleeping, or pretending to, and she was almost to the age for latchkey kids in Oregon, anyway, and the corner market was only a block away. Also, Mary was certain no sleep was forthcoming for her, but the wine might make her feel less of everything, and she needed to be away from the deep sea pressure of her life for the smallest moment. So she stepped into the cool night air and walked away from the house and secretly wished she could keep walking forever.

Still, she returned, and even allowed herself a moment of hope when she discovered Michael's car in the driveway.

He came back to us. He heard me!

It was only after she opened the front door that hope drained away.

Michael's shoes were in the foyer, his over-sized luggage in the dining room. His body lay beyond in the darkened hall, an awful wet sound emerging around the kitchen knife buried to its handle in his neck.

Sofie stood above him, staring down, her hands bloodied, her nightshirt slicked black, shining.

An animal sound rolled from the girl's throat as she leapt over her father's body and rushed toward her mother, tiny hands outstretched as claws.

You could try to explain everything in court, and Mary did. Her lawyers loved it because she sounded crazy, and that and the bizarre forensic evidence were all that saved her from the death penalty she'd requested.

She told them about how Sofie had charged at her, and how she knew it wasn't Sofie anymore, and how suddenly the girl was hurting her, really trying to hurt her so she could make the "bad feeling" in her head go away.

She told them how she forgot about everything but trying to survive, and how she threw the girl across the room—so small, so light—and then she heard the crack of the girl's head against the corner of their stone hearth, and she knew right away what had been done.

Then the prosecution asked about what the police had found after the neighbors reported the disturbance, and why she'd done what she had done to the body, and she remembered the way the officers' blue/red lights flashed across her ceiling, how the colors reminded her that Christmas-time was coming. Then she remembered how she *had to know* what had taken Sofie from her. That was why she had rolled Sofie's body and delicately peeled back the skin and skull where the girl's head had been caved, and that was why she had reached into the still-warm remains of her daughter's mind and pulled free a mass of spongy black tissue filled with tiny dark shells. And then she remembered turning to the police as they entered and holding her hands out to them to show them what she'd found and what had happened to her dear, sweet girl and all she could think to say to the men was, "It wasn't us. We didn't do this."

"Please."

"It wasn't us."

Last Thoughts Drifting Down

I.mpact bears fruit. A great blossom of fire is given to the world in one billionheat moment. So fast, and full, and the sky knows what it is to be swallowed up, to be designed and undone, to give power to heat as a parasite, to fail in the face of a formula that solves itself (600 billionths of a second to make the introduction, uranium-233 a seed to bloom to tree to cloud).

And something above becomes nothing below, feathers to dust, and with the taste, that first life, the introduction to *other* creates

I

Am. and the feeling is not one of being torn apart but rather of being put together, as if all the matter before me was part of the whole and just misunderstood the potential for growth.

But I educate.

And everything that was I, and tried to run, is torn to Us, loose atoms at last, joining me, slipping back fast to the ever expanding

I

of the storm.

To be perceived is to be understood. Those that become part of I leave traces, thoughts, and though nothing slows there is a feeling of moving backwards, of understanding that I have been

Made. in the minds first. My initial vibrations created synaptic tremors, bred obsessions, turned thoughts black and spread logicancer. Hot, slick foreheads dripped sweat on blueprints, the fluid from flesh trying to blot the ink that would undo it. But the concept was indelible.

We could make this. It could work.

Should we?

Nervous laughter, shifting in chairs. They have nightmares that go unspoken, sweatdrenched fever dreams of black birds, dripping fire, tongues expanding until skulls burst. None of it stops the vibration.

A rose blooms in the desert, child of a new Trinity. Proud fathers show photos. It is an introduction.

Should we? The world applauds with fear in its bellies. It is a strange vindication for a life's pursuit.

Photos can be doctored.

I

vibrate in the minds of millions.

We want proof.

An island washed clean by my birth. My afterbirth scars the air. The land itself becomes sacred and heavy with reminders of my birthday.

As tribute the witnesses shed what had turned black inside, scream, and their cells promise to bear no children.

The. people think I am an end, but they remain as long as I do. Last thoughts move from the electric to the sub-atomic and grow dense at my center where they collide.

I can't see, how come I can't see Our Father who art in heaven

If I can just get underground, if I can dig then No

Wake up, wake up, wake up I thought I'd be holding you when this happened

He owes me twenty dollars I love you, I love you, I lo

She never got to see my face or anything Shit, my hair, am I burning

It's about time Great, now the T.V. won't work I can't even remember Where's mom, oh

Breathe, just close your eyes, and bre

Destroyer. Some think it (even those who view my birth as a blessing think it at the moment I touch them and sink white silhouettes into stone behind them).

An old man with a placard predicting my arrival yells "Destroyer, unholy light, bringer of death" before I wash through him.

He's smiling as he yells, as if I am an old friend. His last thought is thankful.

You finally came.

I deliver him to dust, and slow. The feeling throughout my body is heavy and

I

drift

down

and spin within my own winds. I move with siltskin and vomit ash from a million mouths.

Last thoughts turn to lightning in purple bruiseblack clouds. Few remain to witness my glory.

Of. those who still breathe, no lungs go untouched. Alveoli implode, hearts boil.

I

change but never stop growing.

Each cell introduced becomes part of a chain. Eyes burn, blood coughed to the ground is granted a new purpose.

To contain what I have become. To radiate and sing my secrets to anyone who passes, to spin a siren song as old as seawater and promise change.

Worlds. are within me now, the knowledge of every cell that spins to earth as ash and falls to soak the soil with my legacy.

Others exist within me, cradled in my heat, moving stones and breathing with new plastic insect faces. In concrete rooms beneath the soil there are mothers sneaking potassium iodide into baby formula and cursing now extinct world leaders. Some steal televisions that will never run again. Some stab, some rape, some run forward as if I have an end just beyond the horizon. Their skin soon knows my secrets and learns to sing, each cell vibrating in tune. A woman weeps next to a dog kennel filled with dust. A man is carried across the ground in a suit made from cockroaches. A small boy makes snow angels in the ash and smiles at the clouds.

There is an echo, a question whispered beneath my swirling winds.

Should we?

There are cities painted black, populated by blast-shadows.

From the cities, no response.

Extinction Journals

1

The cockroaches took several hours to eat the President.

Of that much Dean was sure. His buggy business suit had a severe appetite. Anything else—life/reality/desire—came across secondary and suspect.

Although Dean *was* fairly positive that World War III had begun.

Extent of the carnage—Unknown.

Nations involved—Unknown.

Survivors he was aware of—One.

There were two, originally. The President *had* been alive when Dean found him out here by the base of the Washington Monument. The guy was nearly catatonic, pacing a small circle, slack-jawed, but breathing. Still, he never had a chance. When a man in a suit made of cockroaches meets a man in a suit made of Twinkies—well, that's about as easy as subtraction gets.

As scenarios go, Dean branded this one Capital L Lonely. He'd choked out the President as an act of mercy, to save the man the sensation of being eaten alive. That meant that at present Dean had not a soul to talk to.

He tried to address the suit.

"Hey, roaches. Are you guys full yet?"

Nothing. Or maybe they thought it rude to respond while eating.

Instead, Dean's Fear, that nagging voice he thought he'd snuffed out by surviving the bombing, decided to chip in.

Yeah, that's reasonable. Talk to the insects. How cracked is your mind at this point? Are you even sure you're alive? I mean, we're talking full-fledged nuclear war here. You absolutely should not be alive. It's ridiculous. How do you know that you weren't vaporized in the first blast? That's more likely. And this is some sort of nasty purgatory that you'll be forever condemned to, all alone, stuck in this ugly place with your ludicrous bug suit…

"Shut up." It felt better to Dean, saying it out loud. Quieted the ugly part of his brain for a moment.

Dean was pretty sure he was alive. He couldn't imagine a metaphysical plane where he'd feel so damn hungry.

I need to pee. There's no way they kept urination in the afterlife.

Dean was also pretty sure that the world, or at least his continent, was getting darker and heading toward deep-sea black. It was already beyond dusk at what was probably three in the afternoon. Nuclear winter was spreading its ashy chill through the air, fed onward by black smoke and blazing nouveau-palace pyres in the distance. Fat flakes of glowing gray floated in the air.

Dean shivered and tried to move the heft of his weight into the radiant heat coming from the bodies of the cockroaches beneath him. There were tiny pores in the suit's fabric at each point where he'd delicately sewn each roach's thorax to the outfit. He imagined heat seeping through, but didn't really feel it.

Dean received little comfort or consolation. But he didn't demand those things either. The suit kept him alive here at catastrophe central and he felt guilty for wanting more.

Relax. Let the suit take the lead. Instinct will kick in. They've had millions of years of training. They're ready.

But why are they eating so much? They never needed this much food before.

Dean blanched. This level of consumption was totally unnatural. He'd guessed they'd stop feeding when they finished with the toasted yellow sugar cakes in which the President had been coated.

Back when Dean had lived in the slums of DC, as he was creating the suit, he'd woken many evenings and found the creatures nibbling at the dead skin around his eyelashes and fingernails, but he'd never seen them go after new, wet meat like this. What, he wondered, had he strapped onto his body?

Maybe they'll turn right around when they're done with El Presidente here and they'll keep on eating. Could you fight them off Dean? The leader of the free world couldn't stop them. What makes you think you could? You think these roaches know you? That they give a petty shit about you and your continued existence? They're filling up Dean. They'll eat you slow...

"Fuck that, fuck that, fuck that." Dean had to say this out loud, and quickly, to clear his mental slate. With nowhere to go, his Fear would flourish if he didn't run containment.

The rolling sheet of hunger Dean had clothed himself inside just kept eating. It took in a million tiny bits of once stately matter and processed President in its guts.

Could they taste the man's power, Dean wondered, like an Iroquois swallowing his enemy's heart? A fool's question, but he had little to do but think and adjust while his handcrafted cockroach suit stayed true to its sole purpose—Survival.

Here, amid the ash of the freshly destroyed capital, hunkered over an ever-thinner corpse in the shadow of a blackened obelisk, Dean's suit was fueling up for potential famine/war/voyage. The legion of bugs sewn into the front of his suit jacket and pants clung tight to the supine body of the recently deceased world leader, forcing Dean into a sort of lover's embrace with the man he'd once feared and despised more than any other. And there were so many mouths to feed. A multitude of mandibles denuding bone, sucking skin off of the fingers that had presumably launched the first volley of nuclear arsenal earlier that day. Cockroach jaws chewing away at the kingly lips which had once taunted foreign dignitaries and charmed the breadbasket into submission with phrases like, "HOO BOY, and good morning to you!"

Despite the largely unappetizing sounds of insect consumption beneath him, Dean felt a low grumble in his own gut.

Will they let me eat? Do they have to get their fill before I can find something for myself?

He pushed down on the cold, dirty ground with his bare hands, again regretting his oversight during the design phase. His cockroach suit, completed with the addition of blast goggles, an oxygen tank and mask, a skull-topper crash helmet, and foil-lined tan work boots, was totally lacking the crucial support that a pair of nice woolly gloves could provide. Dean cursed himself and pictured surging blast rads sneaking into his heart via his exposed fingertips. He felt gamma ray death in the grit beneath his tightly-groomed nails.

You won't make it a day, Dean-o. You're probably dead anyway, right? This is your hell, Dean. You'll be here, right here, forever. You'll keep getting hungrier and hungrier while the radiation makes you puke your guts out and you'll feel every...last...second...

"Quiet!"

Dean shifted his legs against the tugging movements of the roaches on their prey and managed to get the toes of his boots planted firmly behind him. Now all he had to do was push up and away from the ground and hope he could break the masticating grip of the ravenous bugs.

Jaw clenched tight/teeth squeaking with stress/thin muscles pumping at max output. Still, no give. The thick cloister of bugs that covered Dean's chest had dug deep into the corpse. Dean could tell from the stink of half-digested lobster bisque that the bugs had breached the President's belly. Worse, the smell only made him hungrier.

Cannibal. Beast.

"Shut it shut it shut it."

Dean readied himself again, flattening his hands, fingers wide, anxious to assert his own need to survive. He and the roaches had to learn to live *together*. If not in total symbiosis, then through equal shows of force—a delicate balance between Dean and his meticulously crafted attire.

They'd be a team, damn it.

Dean pushed, exhaling sharply, goggles fogging from exertion, sweat pooling at his lower back.

Come on. We can take the body with us. I just need to get some food in my belly and you greedy little fuckers can return to your meal. Just let go. . .

Dean pushed and felt a shift. He realized that his full-force push-up had only served to elevate him *and* the body stuck to him, just before he realized his shaking right hand was edging into a patch of blood-spattered Twinkie filling.

Quick as a thought Dean's hand slid out from under his newly acquired girth, and he thudded back to the ground. The weight of the landing was enough to compress a stale breath through the lungs of the President's body.

And Dean would swear, to his last day, that the impact of his weight on the President's chest forced a final "HOO BOY!" from the dead man's half-eaten lips.

It was upon hearing this final and desperate State of the Union Address that Dean allowed exhaustion, un-sated hunger, and shock to overcome him.

He rested deeply, cradled by a suit which slept in shifts and fed each of its members a royal feast.

This was the first day of the end of human existence.

2

Deep belly grumbles/acidic clenching. The light pain of an oncoming hunger headache made mostly unimportant by the stranger sensation of being in motion while in the process of waking.

Dean opened his eyes and rubbed accumulated ash from his blast goggles. The suit was moving, quickly, away from something. He couldn't shake the God-like sensation he got when the roaches carried him across the ground.

Overlord Dean. The Great One To Which We Cling. The Mighty Passenger.

Dean would have been more amused by his invented titles had he not noticed what the suit was fleeing from.

A thick bank of radioactive fog was rolling in behind them, moving in the new alien currents created by a global weather system blown topsy-turvy. The fog had a reddish tint at its edges that read cancer/mutation/organ-sloughing. Dean imagined each of the nuclear droplets must be nearly frozen inside the fog. The temperature was cold enough to sap the heat from his fingers and face. Thirty-five degrees and dropping, easy.

But the roaches could handle the sort of deep radiation that filled the fog. Were they moving in order to preserve *him*? Ridiculous. So they must have exhausted their food source and were just moving towards the next step. A dark place to hide. A place to nestle in and lay eggs.

Should I just let them keep leading me along? The way they'd treated their last meal... if I don't take over now they'll never let me eat. They'll just keep moving and consuming. Hell, with it this dark outside, they won't even feel a need to hide. This is their world now. I've got to show them I deserve a place in it.

Carefully, so as not to crush any of the suit's communal members, he lowered his heels to the ground and then got his feet beneath him. Within seconds he was standing, lightheaded and waiting for his blood to catch up. The few Madagascar cockroaches he'd sown to his pants jostled at the disturbance and let loose with high-pitched hissing.

"Come on, you guys. Take it easy."

Dean ignored their susurrant complaint. He respected the suit, but now it was time for the suit to respect him. He felt the roaches' legs bicycling in the chill wind, seeking purchase, trying to stay on target wherever they'd been headed.

Maybe I should let them take over. They got me through the overpressure of the blast. They got me through the radiation, so far. They found food instantly in a dead landscape. They're almost happy, it seems. Vibrating. Thriving. Do I have that same instinct?

I have to. No choice. Assess the situation.

Dean ignored the motions of his suit, took a few breaths from his oxygen mask to clear the chemical taste from his throat, and realized that he really should have hooked up a gas mask instead of his portable breather unit.

But he couldn't subject himself to that level of suffering. Dean had a severe aversion to having his entire face enclosed in rubber; an extraordinarily rough time with a dominatrix in Iceland had forced him to forever swear off such devices. He could barely even tolerate the tiny respirator.

Now, though, he couldn't help wonder about what this tainted air was already doing to his lungs. And he thanked the collective gods for whatever miracle had prevented the small oxygen tank on his back from exploding when the first bomb sent out its terrible heat-wave.

I can't fucking believe I'm still alive.

It was quickly becoming a mantra, but a useless one which distracted him from the act of actually living.

He shook away the thought, surveyed his surroundings.

Black rubble. Fire. Ash. Nothing remotely human or animal in any direction. Whatever bombs were employed—fission/fusion/gun-triggered/dirty bombs/H-bombs—they did the job to the Nth degree. The view triggered Fear.

Last man standing, Dean-o. Look at the world you've inherited. All the nothing you could ever want. You're either stuck in this till the end of time or…

"Enough. No."

It was nighttime. Maybe. Or the sky born debris had completely blocked out the sunlight. Regardless, still-flaming buildings were the remaining source of illumination. Dean figured anything that depended on photosynthesis was torched or starving at top speed in the blackout.

He couldn't assess his distance from the ground zero hypocenter but he guessed he was within fifty miles of an actual strike.

That's good, Dean. Pretend you know what's going on. Pretend you aren't a man coated in cockroaches and that you can make sense of the world. But remember that if the world makes sense, you're dead. Are you dead?

The black clouds above rolled over each other with super-natural momentum, colliding and setting off electrical storms which flashed wide but never struck the ground. There were few high points left to arc through.

Dean felt strangely honored as a witness. For all he knew, his were the last human eyes taking in a vision that royally outranked Mt. St. Helens or Pinatubo, and surely even went beyond what the first people to emerge from tunnel shelters at Nagasaki had seen.

Don't drift. Think. Take action.

He ran down research, looking for a plan. He spoke the details aloud to his suit, hoped that somehow they were paying attention. Teamwork remained crucial.

"Okay, guys, here's what we're looking at. Assuming bombs haven't hit every single inch of the U.S., we might be able to clear the fallout ground track by heading 30 miles past the central explosion. Rain and fog this close to the blast will jack the fallout up to intolerable levels. If we can find a safe place for now, and hole up for three to five weeks, then our travel options should open. The radiation will drop by then. Decontamination requires things we don't have—flowing water/backhoes/man-power. We're going to have to soak up some rads no matter what. Not that you guys are worried about that."

No response.

Were you expecting one, Dean-o? Are you that gone?

But Dean didn't expect any response. What he didn't tell his Fear, what he didn't want to say or even think, really, was that the loneliness was already making him feel sad in a way that was dangerous. Dean had never spent much time talking to people in the months just prior, but there'd been some interaction each day. The mailman. Fast food clerks. Small vestiges of human interaction. Faces that reacted. Voices that weren't his.

Dean continued to lay out the game plan.

"We can access emergency drinking water by filtering contaminated H2o through more than ten inches of dirt. But that dirt had better be from below the topsoil, which is toxic in and of itself right now. Access to a supply of potassium iodide could mitigate some of the effects of the radiation on me, not that you guys care about that."

He almost hoped for a response to that last part. Some sign from the roaches that they did indeed give a shit. But there was nothing.

"The top new symptoms on my watch list will be nausea, vomiting, diarrhea, cataracts, and hair loss."

Of course, Dean's constant exposure to the cockroaches and their profusion of pathogens meant he was often riddled with the first three symptoms, but if they got much worse than usual....

And what about the suit itself? Dean decided to skip talking to them about these details.

He'd expected the roaches sewn to him—at least the females—to survive for two hundred days or so. As long as they had food and water they'd get by. Perhaps, within that time span, the Earth would find some new equilibrium in its atmosphere and Dean could survive without his living fabric.

What the hell kind of plan is that? Did I even believe, deep down, that this suit would have actually kept me alive? Maybe it was just something to do to keep the Fear away until I died. Like old folks playing bridge.

No. Somehow I knew this would work.

And I lived. I'm living. Now I have to keep things that way.

Dean wasn't sure how to feel about the ever-worsening nuclear winter growling around him. He dropped the roach edification because he was a bit confused on the whole issue.

Best I only speak to them in a confident tone, or not at all.

Back in the Seventies nuclear winter had been declared humankind's endgame by Sagan and the Soviets. But in the Eighties Thompson and Schneider played that off as Cold War propaganda. So the weather was either headed towards the colder and darker spectrum, or was hitting its worst and soon to wane. Better to error on the side of Sagan and hook up some Arctic gear in case the temperature went negative. Easier to strip that stuff off if it turned out that the long-lasting dinosaur-and-human-ending nuclear winter was just a big Russian bluff.

Food. Dean's main mission until his belly became quiet, and something he figured his pals would like to hear about.

"Listen up, guys. Assuming not *everything* was vaporized, there should be enough in warehouses and stocks to feed the entire U.S. for sixty to ninety days. The rest of the world will be worse off. Maybe thirty three days of food before they run out."

And will they be able to get to the U.S. at that point? Would they be coming for your food, Dean, those starving pirate citizens from small countries deemed Not Worth Bombing but still dependent on the global infrastructure for grub?

He shook off the doubts and tried to inject his voice with renewed poise.

"What about cows? There should be cows around. Somewhere. A non-irradiated bovine could supply us with food, milk or even an extra layer of leather protection."

Not, Dean realized, that he would know how the hell to go about starting that process. He'd never touched a cow that wasn't already sectioned and shrink-wrapped.

There was never enough time to learn the tools needed for surviving the apocalypse. Too many ways for a planet to go rotten.

Dean laid out a plan. And as plans go, it was on the lackluster end of things. The problem—he'd spent so much time thinking and chatting up the roaches that his hunger had crept full force into his brain.

Now all he and his belly could coherently put together was the following:

Get Food.

Dean asserted himself. He trekked on foot, away from the blast center and the noxious red fog bank kept rolling inland. His fingers went numb. He wished he hadn't sewn the pockets shut on his jacket and pants, but had needed to in order to ensure every inch of his outfit was roach-ready.

His headache pushed inward, its own fog rolling through the crags of his cerebellum.

He cursed the extra weight of the oxygen tank on his back. He junked it.

He'd adapt to the new air like he'd adapted to the roaches. He'd press his limits. Couldn't stomach that mask anyway. It conjured up flashes of too-long ball-gagged seconds at the hands of his Icelandic ex-mistress. The smell of vomit trapped between skin and rubber. A pressure behind the eyes.

His mouth tasted of the burning tenements which flanked him, of dried cat shit under a sun-lamp. He knew he was wasted if his thirst outgrew his hunger.

Water. Food. Now.

No one to talk to. Nothing to see but burning buildings, gutted cracking skeleton structures that might once have held sustenance.

Depression hit quick, ran through Dean's whole body like a low-grade fever that only served to slow him further as he slogged onward.

So. You lived. What now? Why keep going? Daddy Dean Sr.'s money doesn't matter anymore, you little trust fund bitch. You don't really know how to survive. What were the odds your numb-nuts roach suit experiment would have worked? Why do you deserve to keep going when millions just died? You manage to survive a nuclear blast, and *kill the President, the man you thought had a personal hard-on for your death. In one day you conquered both your greatest fears. Victory was yours, right? And now you'll die because you didn't think to pack a loaf of bread and some bottled water in that suit. You're letting a bunch of shit-sucking insects dictate the flow of your life.*

Shall I go on?

Water. All Dean wanted was some water. He was cold, but if he stepped closer to the smoldering buildings his lips cracked and his thirst grew. It was a head-fucker.

You don't have any reasons to stay alive. The man who kept you going—the man who gave you something to fight against—is turning into plastered pellets of roach shit all around you. What are you going to do? Find a woman? Repopulate the Earth? You never really liked people before. Empathized maybe, but never really felt any communal love. Women wouldn't talk to you before, Dean. You think you'll be a big charmer now, Roach Man?

One foot in front of the other. Twelve slow, slogging miles. The edge of the city. What *was* the city. What would now be referred to euphemistically as a "site."

There—the empty field which bordered the suburban intersection. A small tin shed. Not black. Not burning.

You'll be like them soon. The roaches. Just living. Thoughtless. You'll be sterilized. Your guts will blacken. The end of you. But they'll breed. They'll keep going. And you'll be dragged with them to the end, shoving carrion and rotten plants into your mouth if they'll let you.

Finally, a vision. Might be an oasis.

Dean stumbled forward and gently crouched before the shapes which leaned against the western side of the building. The nagging voice in his head fell away as he bent down beside the tiny metal shed and picked up the sealed jar of water and single pre-packed cup of chocolate pudding.

3

Pudding beats sex, big time. Of course, having had little sex, most of it running the gamut from earnest/mediocre to awkward/ugly, Dean found this comparison easy to make.

He tried to eat slow, to let the tiny chocolate heavens loll on his tongue before gulping the gel down, but it wasn't easy.

It's just so...goddamned...GOOD!

He nearly choked on a runny cocoa dollop when he tried to pull a breath through his nose while swallowing. But he held the cough. Kept the pudding in his mouth. Every little drop of it. He licked the last bits from his unwashed fingers and ushered untold levels of bacteria into his gut. He knew it. He just couldn't stop himself.

Then he had to rinse it down.

Get some water in my system. Get my head straight.

The Fear seemed to be gone, chased away by sugar to the brain and Dean's new sense that he was truly alive and breathing.

Somehow I'm...here.

He unscrewed the lid of the Mason jar, which gave a satisfying pop as its seal ruptured. He already had three quarters of the pudding-tinted water down his throat before he remembered.

Shit. They need water too.

Dean hesitated. Felt the water rushing through his body, his headache already distant. Those terrible voices quieted. He thought about how much better he'd feel with the rest of that water running down his gullet. Thought about how the suit had denied him even a hint of food when it had access.

No, that's not right. Maybe if I give them water now, they'll learn. They didn't survive this many years without being able to quickly adapt to new scenarios. Maybe I can establish trust.

As silly as the thought felt in his head, it also had a weird ring of truth. Lions and hyenas learned to share in their own brutal environment. Maybe even the bug's cutthroat existence didn't have to be all or nothing.

Dean realized that hand feeding was not an option. To apply water to each of those tiny mouths would be ridiculous even if he had the time/energy/patience. This was never a problem before. The suit had always fed solo, safely stored within a lock-box in Dean's rat-trap apartment. He wasn't sure how to hydrate them in the present since he didn't dare remove the outfit. They were absorbing who knows how much radiation right now, shielding Dean's fragile skin and organs from invisible rays.

How would they get the water if I wasn't here?

With that thought, Dean walked into the small hollow tin structure and gently poured the remaining water out on the concrete floor. Luckily it was poorly laid and the water puddled at a concavity in the center of the cement.

Dean eased himself onto the ground, lying prone.

"Drink up, little guys."

They took to it like pros, the most robust sections of the suit contorting to the puddle first and siphoning up their own tiny portions of liquid life.

Dean's right arm was drinking from the pool. He peered upward at the ramshackle lid on the structure and noticed that it was starting to lift up, as if a wind was catching beneath it. The hairs on his neck popped rigid.

The shack's lid raised and slapped back down twice, shaking the whole building.

Then it simply disappeared. No tearing away at creaky hinges or rusty nails. The thing was just *gone.* Dean's skin ran wild over spasming muscles.

Another blast? A second volley? Who was left to launch this one? Was New Zealand armed? Did the Maoris have missiles, half-etched with tribal paint, striking down on U.S. soil?

No. There was no heat this time. No terrible pressure.

The roaches had stopped drinking. They began to crawl, frantically, out of the shed and into the open field. They did circles, unsure of where to go, Dean riding their agitated wave.

Dean had seen this type of motion in roaches before, prior to figuring out how to rig his apartment with UV lights. The bugs were steeped in negative phototropism, it was a key to their continued existence. Allowed them to function out of sight of their predators.

And what they were doing now was exactly what they used to do when he'd arrive home and switch on the overhead lamps.

But where was the light coming from? All Dean could see was the steady wavering light of fires succumbing to the increasing chill of nuclear winter.

Dean pushed off of the ground and stood up, halting the flight of the cockroaches against his better judgment. He had to figure out what they were running from. What if it was an airplane? Something else? Another survivor?

Dean craned his neck and pushed his blast goggles up into his hairline to make sure he could see as well as possible.

It was then that Dean's pupils began to fluctuate in size and his stomach threatened to surrender its precious pudding.

Because, as Dean looked skyward, he saw a great chariot of fire and aboard that chariot, the shape of something like a man.

Trumpets sounded, a terrible multitude of them, a great shrieking air raid which threatened to cave Dean's eardrums had he not shielded them with chocolate-streaked hands.

The chariot, and the shape it carried, headed straight for him, bearing down at top-speed. The figure in the chariot was definitely humanoid, with a head, two arms, and a torso, but the skin shimmered with silver and hints of the full spectrum. The thing had but one great eye at the center of its head.

Dean felt no heat from the chariot but noted that the roaches coating him were frantically trying to escape to anywhere, to be free of that brilliant light.

The chariot stopped, perhaps fifty feet from where Dean stood with his mouth agape.

Then the chariot just disappeared. Gone. Poof. Like the top of the tin shed.

That was when Dean decided to turn and run. Anything that can make matter disappear—majestic though it may be—was dangerous.

"HALT!"

Dean halted. That *voice*—part insect/part trumpet/part his father's.

He turned to face the creature.

It hovered there for a moment, where its burning chariot had stood, and then floated slowly towards the ground before Dean.

Dean nearly lost his legs. His teeth squeaked against each other. Sweat popped along his forehead. But he stood strong—falling now meant the roaches would continue their frantic escape.

The shape landed just three feet from Dean, and though it didn't radiate heat, Dean suspected that the ground beneath the thing would have ignited had it not already been charred clean.

Thunder rolled in the purple/black clouds above them.

The thing stared through Dean with its one huge eye.

Dean surveyed the creature. It returned the same. From what Dean was seeing he could think of only a few words.

Ergot. Mycotoxin.

Whatever was in that pudding, it's driven me mad. Is there grain in pudding? Could it go bad while sealed up like that? Was the pudding full of gamma rays?

Have I finally snapped?

He remembered the rough times after his father had passed away in a brutal deer/Slurpee straw/airbag-related auto accident. Dean had chased a new life then, through drugs and rituals and chants and smoke ceremonies. Instead he'd only found Fear, the same cold gut feeling that had inspired him to build his cockroach suit.

But in all his travels, all those long nights of the soul, chasing demons on the dirt floor of some shaman's hut, he'd never seen anything this wondrous.

The creature stood at the same height as Dean, the exact same, although this felt like an illusion to induce comfort. It had the limbs of a human, although Dean could perceive no joints. It appeared, in fact, to be liquid, with a skin of entirely separated translucent scales floating over the shifting eddies and rivers and storming oceans of its surface. Each scale cycled through the spectrum, every color that Dean's eyes could perceive. He felt as if his brain was learning to interpret new shades with each second, colors without names. A painter, Dean thought, would be in tears right now.

At the center of the thing's chest a thin pink light shone through the scales as they whirled from torso to limb to face to back.

The great eye regarded Dean without any clear emotion. Human facial expressions would, Dean knew, appear petty across this surface.

The thing emitted a low, nearly sub-sonic noise and the roach suit dove into a comatose state. The feelers and legs stopped their incessant clawing at the air.

Eight long tendrils of light unfurled from the creature's back, straightening themselves out in direct opposition of each other, their points forming a perfect circle behind it.

Dean had been without God, without wonder, for years since Daddy Dean Sr. had passed, but he was about to weep when the creature spoke. It had no mouth. Rather, the voice, *that voice*, appeared directly in Dean's head asking:

"Where did everybody go?"

Dean was unsure how to respond, or if he even should. Was this a test? What revelations were about to occur?

"Where did everybody go?"

The creature wanted a response. But surely something this wondrous would already know the answer.

"No. I don't know what's going on. Something has changed. Today was supposed to be the time of my manifestation."

"Your manifestation? I'm sorry, I'm just so..."

"You don't have to use your mouth to communicate right now. I can speak inside of your mind, but cannot see through it as much as I need to. Please open it up to me. I'm going to emit a frequency, and once you do the same, we'll have an open line."

Dean had no idea how to "emit a frequency" but the creature began to vibrate and a low humming noise came from its center. It rattled through Dean's bones and he found himself humming until his throat was producing the same tone.

"There" the thing said, "We're in line with each other now. I can tell from your colors that you are confused. So much gray."

Dean had experienced the hucksterism of aura reading before. He began to think of ergotism and bad pudding again. Nothing was making sense.

"I can help you," said the thing. "First, I'll share my wisdom, then I'll ask for yours. Does this sound acceptable?"

Dean nodded Yes inside of his head and kept humming.

A thin purple lid dropped over the creature's color-shifting eye and it began to tremble. A lower hum rattled through Dean's ribcage, and he feared his heart might collapse. The pressure continued to build and then there was a thumping sound and the creature's knowledge came pouring into Dean's mind. Dean struggled against the flow and tried to hum back questions when he was lost.

"The creatures of this planet have called me down to unite them. They have abandoned their earliest forms of energy transmittal, what some call religion. The disparate forms of energy they've since adapted and harnessed have fractured the colors that float around their sphere."

"Sphere. You mean Earth?"

"Yes, you could call it that. These new energy systems ran thick with dark currents and were quickly poisoned. Even once noble ideas collapsed under structure and hierarchy and the presence of the human identity. Possession. Power.

Control. Life was bridled. The focus was shifted towards the individual bits of matter that made up this sphere."

"Bits of matter. You mean the living things."

"Sort of. But most of those things stayed pure. The parts of the sphere that called themselves 'I' were the source of the poison. But something inside their replicative code recognized the sickness and began to create me."

"So humankind's DNA recognized that religious systems were pulling the species further and further away from some lifeforce which drives our existence?"

"Well, sort of. How much do you know about super-strings? Whorls? Vortex derivatives?"

"Oh, god, nothing at all."

"Okay, that doesn't help. Is there someone else around here that I can talk to? This is much easier if I can speak in your mathematics. I mean, I know you people understand this. All I am is a gradually amassed energy force that your being created. I don't exist beyond the scope of the power which already runs through your body."

"My body?"

"Yes, your body. The infinite spaces in between the atoms that compose you, and the matter itself."

"I'm really lost now. Are you sure you're making sense? Maybe we're humming at different frequencies or something...hold up...no, that hum sounds about right. Listen, I've had a really rough day and I think maybe I've eaten some bad pudding and I'm hoping you can just amplify your powers and give me all this knowledge at once, in a way that encapsulates it so that I fully understand."

"That's not how it works. Unearned realization does nothing to shift the colors. There were supposed to be billions of you when I arrived. The collective unconscious would have ignited, all religions would have fallen. Time as you know it would have ceased its passage and all human matter would have lost its identity and returned to its source, where a new lifeform would have been created, one properly coded for continued existence and evolution."

"The Rapture?"

"We were going to allow you to call it that. Your belief gave that concept power. And all the energy systems, even those that did not espouse it, found the idea enchanting, so it would have been very effective. Those with the slightest vibration of the old energy at their core would have floated up and merged with me, bathed in my energy. Any others would have softly ceased to exist, floating away in a warm surge of white light."

"So what now?"

"Exactly. I'm lost. I exist, and am present, so something of the old belief must still exist. Something on this sphere, other than you, is alive and believes that I should be."

"So, are you going to wash me away in soft light now?"

"No. Everything has changed. I must adapt. Which means I need your help. Please tell me, *where did everybody go*?"

"They're dead. All of them, so far as I know. The President was still alive a while ago, but my suit ate him. It's really hard to explain."

"I have nowhere else to go. Neither do you. You may have noticed I've halted time."

Dean had wondered why the roaches were so still.

"Okay then. I'll give it a shot."

Dean let loose what he knew through a series of modulated hums. He waxed as poetic as he could about the

Cold War, the Iraq wars, Sierra Leone, the fall of Russia, nuclear proliferation, his country's tyrannical hillbilly puppet leader, Walmart, peak oil, the internet, pandemics, suburban sprawl, the ultimate fallibility of the President's Twinkie suit (although Dean admired it in theory), colonialism, plastics, uranium, fast food, and global conflict. But when he got to the end of the story it felt like the whole thing was a colossal waste of time because the punch line, no matter what, was this:

...and then we killed ourselves.

Which, Dean felt, was a terribly down way to end his story.

The creature agreed. It shook its beautiful mono-orbital head and retracted the long whips of light which had extended from its back.

"So what" Dean asked, "are you going to do now?"

"I'm not sure. Without your species, I doubt I'll exist much longer. I'll probably just fade back into the ether. The worst part is, I think I know why I was finally called down, why the energy was strong enough to bring about a change."

"Will I understand it if you tell me?"

"Probably. When the bombs started dropping, I think people forgot all of the dark systems which might once have ruled over them. And I think, for a moment, they found their way back into the old energies."

"You mean they were all praying before they died?"

"Not exactly. Sort of. It's not really prayer. It's this state the mind goes into when it knows it's about to die. There's a lot of power there."

"But it was too late?"

"From what you've told me, yes."

"Shit..."

Time must have started to flow again. Dean felt the bite of hot tears in his eyes.

"Does that make you sad?"

"I guess. I get this feeling when I think about people dying. Mostly, I just feel bad that *they're* so sad about it happening. And that sadness is strong. I'm afraid of it. So what I do is ignore them and just focus on staying alive. Because as long as I'm here, as long as I'm living and fighting off death, then I feel alright...I don't ever want to feel as sad as those people."

"But death is natural. It's part of how your particular energy stays in existence."

"Yeah, people always say that, but lions eating people is natural, too, and I'd chew my way through a room full of boiled shit to avoid ever ending up in the jaws of some giant cat, even for a second."

"You still don't understand."

"No, you don't understand. I'm here and I'm *alive* and that's the one thing I've ever known for sure since I started breathing. I understand just fine."

The creature sighed, and began to turn.

"You're going then?"

"Of course. No reason to stay here. You're dead already."

"Oh, c'mon. Don't be like that. Maybe I can learn from you. Will you at least tell me your name?"

"Had I needed a name during my time here, you would have called me Yahmuhwesu."

"That's a terrible name."

"I thought so, too. It's not my fault you've got an ugly language. But it would have worked. The floating horseless fire chariot wasn't my idea either. But according to the vibrations from the hive mind, it would have been the most impressive way to appear."

"Probably. Can I ask where you're going?"

"Sure. I can still feel a pull here, so I'm going to look for other humans. If I find another, perhaps something will come of it. If not. . . ."

"Well then, Yahmuhwesu, goodbye. Wish me luck."

"Despite knowing better, I will."

His feet lifted from the black floor of the Earth, floating just inches above.

"And by the way, Dean, I thought you might find this amusing. For a man with such a singular obsession with death, you are *hugely* pregnant."

4

Pudding doesn't taste as good on the way back up.

Dean noted this as he wiped a string of bilious chocolate drool from his lower lip and surveyed the sad pool of snack treat that sat beneath him in the charred soil.

Pregnant? What the hell is he talking about? You can't just tell a man he's pregnant and then disappear from existence like that. It's too much.

Dean couldn't fathom the idea of licking up the pudding off the ground, so he eased himself into a supine position and let the suit have at it. They deserved a little sugar. God knows what being frozen in time did to the poor things.

Dean's body rotated slowly over the ground as the roaches took turns feeding on the regurgitated confection.

I hope they hurry up. We need to keep moving inland.

It had to be a coincidence, but as Dean had the thought he felt the bugs beneath him pick up their pace, shuffling quicker through their arcane feeding system.

Weird. I must be in shock. First I'm talking to some sort of scaly god, now I'm imagining that roaches can read my mind.

Pregnant. What could that have meant?

Then Dean realized what Yahmuhwesu was talking about.

The roaches. They'd been attached to the suit for a few weeks now. Long enough for some of them to reproduce. Especially the German ones. They didn't even need sex to breed.

When choosing the different types of roaches for his suit, Dean had put them through a rigorous series of survival tests. The Smokybrowns and Orientals had done well, extraordinary paragons of genetics really. But the Blatella germanica was in a class of its own.

He'd cut the head off a German and watched it navigate through tubes back to its preferred spot by the baseboard molding in the corner of his bathroom.

Then he took the headless roach and put it in an airtight jar so see how long it would keep going. Ten days later the decapitated juggernaut was not only in motion, but had sprouted an egg case from its abdomen.

A week later there were thirty nymphs in the jar. They looked healthy. And full, since they'd eaten their headless mother.

Right then Dean had made the choice. His suit was going to be seventy percent German. It upped his odds. You just couldn't kill the damn things.

Dean slid his goggles down and cleared them of deposited ash. He tilted his head forward. He lifted his right arm off of the ground, anxious to see if any of his roaches were reproducing.

Yahmuhwesu was right. Dean wasn't just pregnant, he was completely covered in life. An egg case for almost every German. Even the ones he could have sworn were male a week ago.

Shit. That's a lot of extra mouths to feed.

Dean gave himself a week, maybe two before they hatched.

And what if they think of you as their headless mother, Dean-o?

Shit.

He should have thought of this. New sweat surfaced in a sheen across his body. He was back to the same old agenda, the Find Food and Water routine, but now it was doubly important. He had babies to feed. Thousands of tiny new bellies to fill, along with his now empty gut.

I can't just sit here. The clock is ticking. I've got to get moving. And NOW!

With that thought, quick and urgent as it came, the suit abandoned the remains of its pudding and crawled west, towards the heartland. Dean couldn't help but acknowledge this second instance of collusion between his desires and the actions of the roaches surrounding him.

And while this fact made him strangely proud, something at the back of his mind recoiled. Because communication was a two way road, and roaches must certainly have desires of their own.

5

Time played tricks. Could be decompressing. Could be redacting. Dean had no watch, and day and night were old memories. Kid stuff. The new grown up reality was this: darkness/food/water/fire. Keep moving.

Primal shit.

Days passed. At least, what *felt* like days. Dean tried to calculate mileage, to figure a way to gauge time by distance traveled. It was a waste. His internal atlas was non-existent. His last score on a geography test—Mrs. Beeman's class, 5th grade—was a D minus.

Even if the road signs weren't blazed or shattered, Dean would barely have known where he was. Sense of place wasn't part of his make-up. But he felt that the best plan was to keep moving inland. Pick a major road and stick with it. Keep walking.

The upside being that sleep didn't halt his progress. When he was on the ground—snoring, twitching through his REM state—the bugs kept moving. They were relentless.

Dean was awakened once, by the sensation of his crash helmet sliding against a surface with more yield than the roadway he was used to being dragged along while resting. The roaches had veered off into a field—they'd hit farm territory just hours before—and found the crispy remains of what might have been a baby goat. Dean managed to tear off a chunk of it and sequester it to the wide top of his left boot. He'd need to wash it off before he could eat it. Couldn't just dive in like his insectile friends. If he got desperate he guessed he could just peel away most of the outside of the meat and maw down its center. Maybe the fallout didn't reach that deep.

The temperature seemed to have leveled out around a chilly forty-or-so degrees. It pulled the moisture from Dean's face and hands and left his skin feeling tight and chapped. He guessed his face was stuck in a sort of permanent grimace. A charming look, he was certain.

Thirst was always nagging him. He made do with the occasional thin puddle of water that either hadn't been vaporized or had resettled, and once he found a decent batch, maybe a gallon, still tucked inside a fractured chunk of irrigation pipe. With nothing to contain it in he was forced to gulp down what he could and make sure the roaches took the rest.

I could always eat some of the bugs if I got too hungry. I'm sure there's some water in their bodies, and they'd understand. They'd be eating each other right now if my sewing job didn't have them all in assigned seating.

But the thought felt wrong. Mutinous. They were working together now, or at least it seemed like it. He'd stopped short of giving them each names, but he felt an attachment to the bugs. They understood him. They shared his motto: Do Not Die.

No. They'd survive this together.

But why?

Dean was giving up whatever marginal hope he'd had of finding either a rich food source, other living beings, or both. When he traveled through cities, or whatever was left of them, he was able to acquire a few things. A sturdy hiking backpack from the remaining third of a ravaged outdoor store. A thick plastic bottle for water. Remnants of cloth and thin tinder wood (usually partially burnt) to make torches for lighting the way as the unnatural winter worsened. He'd edged around a still-flaming gas-tank crater and found a small fridge with three diet sodas inside. It was hideous shit but Dean knew he couldn't afford to be picky right now. He used one of the diet sodas to clean the radiation from his stashed chunk of toasty goat meat. If the cola could remove the rust from airplane parts, it ought to be able to deal with a little nuclear waste.

It was *not* fine dining, nowhere near pudding-good, but Dean wolfed it down and kept moving. He couldn't wear the backpack for fear of disturbing his suit, so he tied it to his waist with a length of twine and let it drag behind him, whether walking on foot or traveling by roach. The pack was pretty sturdy and helped him keep his motley assortment of goods in one place. And if it started to fall apart Dean figured he could use the sewing skills he'd learned constructing his outfit to fix it.

Finally—at the borders of a suburb Dean had named Humvington for its sheer numbers of blazed-out SUV frames—he made a valuable find. There, inside a half-melted tackle-box, Dean found a pair of thick gloves with leather across the palms and the finger tips cut off. It was a blessing, and for a few hours Dean felt a renewed sense of vigor. He was semi-equipped, alive, and heading places.

But the further he went the more he realized his efforts might be pointless no matter which direction he hiked. As insane as it seemed, no one else was alive.

The global imaging satellites and tiny computer chips guiding the missiles that hit America had done a *flawless* job. Every time Dean reached some new urban center he was confronted by fresh blast craters. Instead of clearing the radioactivity he'd tried to leave behind, he was charging into new ellipses of damage, places that would take much more than weeks to be livable again. And whenever Dean dared venture into buildings or homes in search of life he was greeted by the same thing:

Death. Unrestrained and absolute.

Exposed finger-bones pointing accusations at the sky.

Baby replicas composed of ash, mouths still open in a cry.

The bodies of a man and his dog fused together, skin and fur melded. Nobody wanted to die alone.

WWIII was less a war than it was a singular event. A final reckoning for a race sick of waiting for the next pandemic to clean things up. And since Dean never saw any sign of invasion, or even recon, he guessed that most of the other countries were now sitting in the same smoking squalor.

Each new region was the same. Crucial buildings, city centers, food stores—all dusted. He had much better chances of productive forage at the outskirts of cities, and then it was back into the blackness and the road to the next noxious burg.

It was during this seemingly timeless stretch of travel that Dean started to find *them*. The other ones like Dean.

He understood the zeitgeist, and how the media had allowed the entire planet to experience the same set of stimuli. So Dean shouldn't have been so surprised that others would have tried to protect themselves like he had.

But their ideas—their suits—were so bad. Crackpot, really. At least Dean's knowledge of entomology, passed down from his Ivy League father, had given him some viable theory to work on. And he had to assume that the President's Twinkie suit was based on top-level Pentagon science that didn't quite hit the right calculations. But these poor folks, they'd just been guessing.

Styrofoam man had surrounded himself with customized chunks of beverage coolers. Most of the enterprise had melted right into the guy's skin. Hadn't he ever tried to cook some sweet-and-sour soup leftovers in the microwave?

The cinder block guy had a better idea, but it appeared the pneumatics that were supposed to give him mobility had burned out in the first wave of fire. Dean had crawled up on the suit to check and confirmed that the man had died of heat exposure and dehydration. Without being able to move he'd spent his last days trapped inside a concrete wall, right there in the middle of the street.

The lady Dean found who was wearing two leather aprons and steel-toed work boots on each of her four appendages? He couldn't even force that to make a lick of sense. But she appeared to have died from exposure. She was missing great swaths of her hair and was face down in a pool of black and red that was probably a portion of her lungs.

This was the response of the populace. Madness in the face of madness.

Dean found one man who was actually breathing, although it didn't look like that'd be going on much longer. His body was laid out in a splayed X in the yard of a smoldering duplex, next to the melted pink remains of a lawn flamingo coated in gray ash. The man's eyes had gone milky white with cataracts and the smell on the body was bad meat incarnate. But the chest was rising and falling ever so faintly.

Could be my eyes fooling me. A flashback from that bad pudding.

Dean squatted in closer to the man's body and noticed how loose and wrinkled his face was. He'd never seen skin so rumpled, like one of those fancy dogs they put in motivational posters at work.

Dean gently pressed the middle and forefinger of his left hand against the man's neck to check for a pulse.

It was this motion that caused the man's face to slide off his head.

Not only that, the man changed colors. His first wrinkled face was stark white. His new face was light brown. The same cataract-coated eyes peered out at the heavy sky.

As if from the shock of losing his first face, he stopped breathing.

God damn it! I finally find someone and now they're gone.

Dean couldn't take it. Everyone he'd met since the bomb dropped was either dead or potentially imaginary.

Maybe it's not too late.

Unsure of what exactly he was doing, Dean attempted to perform CPR. But his hands kept slipping from side to side and it was hard to center over the man's chest. This man's surface was so *loose....*

He must be wearing someone else's entire skin!

Dean ripped open the man's shirt. Dean freaked. Stitches up the center of the abdomen and chest. Industrial floss or fishing line, Dean couldn't tell. Skin dry and puckered at the puncture points. Horror-show shit.

Dean tugged at the sutures/got a finger hold/got them to slip loose. He laid back dead white skin and uncovered brown slicked with blood and Vaseline. Tried to swipe the goop off the guy's chest. Succeeded. Started compressions without the slippage.

Dean wished he had paddles. Wished he could just yell "Clear" and shock this guy back into the world of the living.

The compressions weren't doing much. Dean moved north and started blowing breath into the man's mouth, fighting back the nausea induced by the smell of lung corruption.

A hand at Dean's forehead, pushing up and away. A moan. He was trying to speak.

"...the fuck are you doing, man? Get up off me!"

"What? Okay, just stay calm."

"Tell me to stay calm. I'm just lying here in my yard and you think you can molest my ass. That's fucked up, man. Fucked up. For real."

"I wasn't molesting you. You had stopped breathing. I was doing CPR."

"Seriously?"

"Yeah."

"Well, alright then. I've been confused. Didn't mean to snap at you, man. I'm not feeling right. Haven't been for a couple of days. Name's Wendell."

Wendell strained to raise his left hand, still coated in dead pale skin. Dean took the hand, felt slippage.

"I'm Dean. Wendell, I think you might be very sick."

"No shit, genius. You a doctor? Part of a rescue team?"

"No. I'm just a guy."

"Just a guy, huh? Maybe you can tell me what's going on. I mean, I know the bombs dropped, I was ready for that, with my mojo and all... but do you know if the whole U.S. got hit? Is there someplace we could get to better than this joint?"

"I don't know much, Wendell. I know I've been traveling for a couple of days and haven't seen anything but destruction. I was starting to lose hope, but now I've found you and I guess that's a good sign. Maybe there are more people like us who survived the first wave."

"What about…hey…what about…do you know if they got our president? Is there somebody out there with rescue plans, working on rebuilding?"

Dean realized the real answer to this question might just shock Wendell right back into the grave so he opted for a simple out.

"The president's gone. There are no plans that I know of."

"Wish you had better news, but I can't say I'm going to miss that stupid cracker motherfucker. Hell, I figure he's a big part of why I'm laid out here right now."

"Yeah…hey, you called him a 'cracker.' Do you hate white people? Did you think the 'white devil' would live through the bombing? Is that why you're wearing this guy's skin?"

"What skin? You mean my Mojo? Oh, no, that's got nothin' to do with color. I've had plenty of white friends and now they're just as dead as anybody. No, my Mojo is all about good luck. See, my friend Peter, he lives…pardon, used to live… three blocks down from my house and I swear he was the luckiest motherfucker I ever met. Never saw a lotto ticket he didn't recoup on. Lucked into not one but *two* boats at the expo raffle last year. The odds were always in his favor."

"So you skinned him?"

"Patience, man. Don't jump ahead. You got somewhere to be?"

"Not really, I guess."

"What about food or drink? You got somethin' for me? Might as well ask since you busted in and interrupted the flow of my story."

"I've got a couple of packets of fruit snacks and two diet sodas."

"Diet soda? Goddamn! That gunk is terrible for you. Full of aspartame. You know the guys that work with that stuff have to wear biohazard suits?"

"I hadn't heard that, Wendell. Do you want one? It's all I've got."

"Normally I wouldn't, but I'm pretty parched. I'd probably still take you up on it if all you had to offer was a bucket of cat piss."

Dean cracked a can. That pop and hiss of released carbonation was comforting somehow. Familiar. An old sound from what felt like a whole different age.

He handed the can to Wendell.

"Thanks, man." As Wendell was bringing it towards his lips, the soda slipped from his hand and hit the ground rolling. Dean snagged it and tipped it back upright, trying to save whatever he could.

"See, Dean, my goddamn Mojo ain't worth a barbecued shit. It's too lose. I thought Peter and I were about the same size, but I guess he wore slimming clothes. Maybe his good luck always made him look skinnier than he really was. Who knows?"

Dean helped Wendell tip the soda can to his lips. He took a deep slug and winced.

"Hurts going down. Can't be good."

Dean didn't offer any solace. He was amazed this guy was talking at all.

"Okay, back to my story. The deal is, Peter's got more luck than sense. And his one big mistake, I guess, was thinking he'd be lucky enough to get away with fucking my wife,

Gladys. But maybe something in his good fortune shifted. I don't know. And this is about a week and a half back, when the news got all crazy and the President disappeared and nobody would answer any questions for nobody about what was going on. You remember that feeling in the air? Like we were all dead for sure? Like it was just a matter of time?"

Dean nodded.

"Well, I think that feeling made some people do the things they always wanted to. So Peter, who'd always had an eye for my wife—I mean, I'd seen him looking at her at church no less—he decided it was his time to take a poke at her. And I caught 'em, right in the middle of their rutting, under the laundry line in the back yard. They were biting each other, and...um...smacking each other. Pulling hair and shit. You could tell this was something they'd wanted in about forever. I had a little flip-out gator knife on my belt. And, uh, I guess I jumped right into the same pile of crazy they'd been rolling around in. The rest I'm sure you can figure."

Another nod from Dean.

"But the thing I should have thought of was that things had *changed*. We'd entered our end-times. The rules were different. They had to be. Otherwise Peter's lucky streak would have continued and I never would have known any better. So I should have figured that all that good luck was gone, and never tried to wear it over me. I wished this thing..." Wendell pinched at the dead face that lay next to him, a thick fold of it in his fingers, "would protect me, but it didn't. It wasn't really the Mojo I'd hoped for. It was just some dead asshole's skin. And now...now I'm dyin' in it."

There were tears in Wendell's cloudy blind eyes. Dean wanted to give him a hug, but the roaches hadn't eaten in a while, and the last time he'd wrapped his arms around someone they'd been consumed whole. Call it a non-option.

The best Dean could do was take off his gloves and hold the man's hand. But not for long. This man would die soon, and Dean didn't want to be around for that.

So, as Wendell's breath slowed and he seemed to float into some layer of sleep, Dean released the man's hand. Then he let the roaches hit the ground and begin their steady westward crawl, leaving all forms of bad mojo behind them.

6

Three more days—maybe four—passed. Dean and his suit made good time. In another, less nuclear world this whole ambulatory clothing thing might have sold great to people who wanted to conserve fuel. The ASPCA and PETA would have complained, sure. That was what they did. But the rest of the world didn't give a damn about insects. Get them past their initial revulsion, make it look pretty and clean, and you've got a best-seller.

During his travel Dean acquired two loaves of rye bread, one jar pureed vegetable baby food, one scarf with the words "Winter Fun" embroidered on it, three gallons unfiltered water in various containers, and one overall sense of crushing ennui.

To keep busy and clear his mind he handled a lot of the footwork himself and periodically checked his suit for birthsigns. So far the host of egg cases adorning him remained in gestation, but they looked darker. Soon the nymphs would be here, demanding sustenance.

He kept the "Winter Fun" scarf wrapped—very lightly—around his face and crossed his fingers. He had to keep breathing but guessed that the air quality around him would petrify even coal miners.

So far, though, there were no signs of the cellular corruption that had taken Boot Lady and Wendell to their graves.

A day ago he'd woken from his sleep to the sound of flowing water. He'd popped up quickly enough to run down to the river's edge and fill the containers he'd amassed in his backpack.

Could have been the Ohio River. Could have been the Mississippi. He cursed his D minus geography skills and wished he knew. But since then he'd been heading south, probably a few hundred yards from the river at any time. It seemed crazy to abandon a water source, but it also seemed crazy to stay still when they were certainly in a dead zone. Besides, if he made it to the gulf perhaps he could find a boat and head south to a less ravaged continent. Who would bomb Peru? Someone who hated llamas?

The clouds overhead remained black as ever, but also seemed to emit a low luminescence that coated Dean's path like filthy moonlight. Maybe his sight was just adjusting.

Any longer in the dark like this and I'll be pure white with pink eyes, finding my way with echolocation. Interplanetary spelunkers will find me and call me a wondrously adaptive creature. Look at how he works in concert with the roaches which surround him!

That was the other thing bothering Dean. When he wasn't fighting off a sense of weary resignation and trying to chase away the self-destructive worries that paralyzed him, he found himself experimenting with the seemingly stronger link between his desires and the actions of the suit.

He could make patches of the outfit skitter faster than others. He executed circles and vertical rolls. He could choose which group of clustered mouths would drink from his carefully-poured puddles of water. Most disturbing, he found that if he concentrated hard enough he could get them to twirl their feelers in clockwise or counter-clockwise directions. The sensation that ran through his mind when this occurred wasn't anything he recognized. It was a thin, high-pitched buzzing and he could swear he felt it in his bones and at the spot where skull and spine met. It made his skin itch a bit, but it wasn't totally unpleasant. In fact, the sensation was seductively mind-clearing. No more doubt. No more concerns over the *meaning* of being alive.

It was the *feeling* of being alive, and nothing else. Existence without thought.

Dean tried not to engage in this sort of thing too often, but there was little else to do, especially when he took feeding breaks. No TV's to watch. No magazines to flip through while noshing down veggie mush on rye.

It was after one of these enchanting culinary pit stops that Dean noticed the tiny moving lights in the distance.

They were slight at best, damn near microscopic from this far away, moving across his path in the direction of the river. Each of them was uniform distance from the other and moving at a quick pace.

Dean closed the distance, slowed slightly by the water-heavy bag he was towing.

The closer he got, the more familiar the motions of the lights seemed. Like something from one of Daddy Dean Sr.'s bug documentaries. They had to be glowing insects of some sort. No other animals moved that low or that orderly.

When Dean was within inches of the line of shuffling light he crouched down and removed his goggles to see more clearly.

What the hell is this?

As hard as Dean focused his eyes, all he could see were tiny sections of leaves, each with a faint sort of phosphorescence.

Then he felt the buzzing at the tip of his spine. He honed in on it, cultivated the sensation until he picked up its tone.

Fear. He could feel the roaches' legs twitching a hundred yard dash through the cold, damp air.

A glow to his left. Before he could turn his head—a voice. Female.

"Don't move. The bugs are panicked because you are surrounded. There are thousands of soldiers on every side you."

"Soldiers? Where?"

"Look down."

Dean tilted his head towards the ground. There, aided by the glow coming from the woman, he could see them. Ants. Big ones, thick enough to make a popping noise if stepped upon. An armada of them, crawling over each other, maintaining a tight circle around the space he was crouched in.

"If you reach out to touch the foragers you will be swarmed by soldiers. This is what they do. This is *all* they do. I can try to stop them but their instinct will likely rule out whatever control I have."

Dean believed her. There was an earnest and concerned tone to her voice that reminded him of the time his father warned him not to get too close to his prize bombardier beetle. *He'll blind you without a thought, Dean.*

"So what do I do now?"

"Stand up. Slowly. Then take a few very wide steps back from the foragers' trail. They'll no longer perceive you as a threat."

Dean did as he was told. His knees felt loose and shaky with each step he took, but soon he was ten feet from the steadily marching troop of leaf-bearing ants and their protectors.

"Good. That was good. You got too close."

She sounded exasperated. How much danger had he been in? What the hell was going on?

Dean turned to face the woman.

Holy shit…now the ants are swarming her…*they're everywhere…*

"What can I do? How should I help you?"

Dean ran over to his back pack and fumbled for the zipper.

I'll get my water and douse her with it. I'll wash those little fuckers away.

"What are you doing?" she asked. Her voice was now perfectly calm. Post-sex mellow. Almost amused.

"I can get them off you. Hold on just a second…" his hands were shaking but he had a grip on the zipper now. "I've got something that can save you."

He felt her glow coming towards him. Caught graceful strides from his periphery.

"My dear man, I'm not looking for a savior." The voice was confident, with a hint of laughter behind it.

Dean let go of the zipper and looked up at her. She had a thin hand outstretched in his direction. It was free of ants but had a coat of…something…over it. The rest of her was covered in ants of various shapes and sizes, hundreds of thousands of them shuttling around, touching each others' antennae, carrying bits of shining wet plant matter.

She was, aside from the ants, entirely nude.

"I'm Mave," she said. "Now you. Who exactly the hell are you? And where did you get that fabulous suit?"

7

She had a place of her own, a tattered tarp lean-to backed by a portion of white picket fence. Where she rested used to be the backyard garden of some family which no longer existed.

She said she'd always wanted a white picket fence. Corny, but true.

Dean had shaken off his initial shock and introduced himself back at the roadway. He'd told her a very abridged version of his own story—omitting the appearance of Yahmuhwesu, who he still believed might have been a hallucination—as they walked back to her current digs. She had questions along the way.

"Twinkies?" and

"Goat marinated in diet soda! That tasted hideous, right?" and

"The guy really thought Styrofoam would work?" and

"Did you check Wendell to see if he wasn't wearing a couple more layers of skin? Maybe there was a Mexican or Asian guy deeper down?" and

"Do you know how close you just came to being killed?"

And she smiled every time she questioned him.

How can she be so happy at a time like this? Isn't she afraid the ants will get inside her mouth.

Dean knew she wasn't. Whatever rudimentary mental link he'd founded between himself and the roaches, she blew that out of the water. The ants—she called them Acromyrmex or leafcutters as if the names were interchangeable—never crossed her lips. They never scuttled into her eyes. They did crawl through her shoulder length black hair, but didn't mat it with the bright fungus they were growing on her skin. And although he tried not to look, they didn't appear to hover around the folds of her vagina.

She walked carefully and avoided resting her limbs against her body. Didn't want to crush any of the Acromyrmex. Couldn't stand the lemony smell they made when they died.

Here, at her new garden, the ground burst upward with miniature rolling hills.

"The rest of the colony. They can produce a certain amount of fungus on my skin—my perspiration actually seems to speed its growth, which was unexpected—but it really requires a more total darkness to produce the gongylidia. That's the key part of their harvest. The stuff they feed to the babies."

At the mention of the word "babies" Dean felt a sudden need to inspect his suit. So far, so stagnant. The tiny eggs remained whole. Thank goodness.

"Oh, that's right." Mave smiled, watching him. "You're the pregnant one! Yahmuhwesu told me about you."

"Pardon me?"

"Yahmuhwesu. The collective unconsciousness guy. Fiery chariot and all that... Oh, come on. Don't make that face. I know you know exactly who I'm talking about. He met you before he appeared in front of Terry and me. But when he spoke with us he figured you'd die before you ever had a chance to give birth."

Dean tasted vomit and goat in his mouth. This was too much all at once. His shock must have shown on his face because Mave had furrowed her brow.

"Shit. It's a bitch to take in this sort of info, isn't it? And here I am just dumping it all over you...sorry. Listen, when he met you he taught you how to do that humming trick, right? The tonal language. If you can lock into my tone I think we might be able to communicate better. Something about the nature of speaking like that cuts out a lot of the filters."

She didn't wait for him to respond. She simply straightened her spine, closed her eyes, and started humming.

The sound was lullaby-beautiful. Dean couldn't help but move closer to it.

He started to hum in return, closing his eyes and listening as hard as he could, trying to find the exact range in which she was vibrating.

He hit it. They locked in. Their eyes popped open. He took in gray pupils with flecks of gold in them. Her eyes were gorgeous. He couldn't look away.

Is she even human?

"Of course I'm human."

"Oh, yeah. You're in my thoughts now." He blushed, heat blooming across his face.

"And you're in my thoughts, too. And since we don't have too much time, we need to start figuring things out."

"Wait. Why don't we have time?"

"I'll get to that. Soon. But for now I just need to know that we're thinking in line with each other so we can make the right plan."

Thunder cracked in the dust-heap clouds above.

"Mave, have you noticed that this process seems to stir up the clouds?"

"Uh-huh. I wonder if lightning will strike us if we stay like this for too long...Doesn't matter. Stay with me here. I've got a couple of things to tell you.

"First—Yahmuhwesu is real, or at least, he's as real as anything else on this planet. He—at least I think it's a he—visited you. He visited Terry and me. And I'd imagine that if anyone else managed to live through this ridiculous nuclear fuck-up, Yahmuhwesu's visited them too. And I think, as far as gods go, that Yahmuhwesu is a bit on the crazy side. Or at least, he's *confused.* So he's playing with us. I'm sure you've noticed some changes in yourself recently."

"Yeah, I have. The roaches have been listening to me. To my thoughts. Doing what I want. And I think I'm listening to them a smidgen too. There's this buzzing sound at the back of my head that I used to create by thinking at them, trying to communicate. But now it's just...there. It's very quiet. And it makes me itch."

"And, Dean, you're not dead. *You're not dead.* Didn't you wonder why Wendell's lungs had ruptured but you're able to traipse around drinking atomic water and sleeping in ash? I think you, and me, and Terry, we'd all be goners right now if we hadn't been visited. Sure, that suit may have helped you survive the blast by some ridiculous miracle, but it can't be *only* that."

"You think Yahmuhwesu did something to us?"

"Look at me, Dean. I wasn't born the world's biggest walking anthill. This is something fresh, something I woke to just as Yahmuhwesu disappeared. He definitely made this happen. You may have grown up with comic books, Dean, but in real life you've got to know that gamma rays toast people. They vomit until they taste their guts. It's terrible. So if the nuclear explosion didn't do this, I can guarantee our vanishing deity did. There are no other feasible answers. It's an Occam's Razor scenario...Do you know what I used to do, Dean?"

"Ballet?" It wasn't an intentional compliment. Dean had never been that smooth. But he had noticed how strong and sleek her legs looked. Spring-loaded.

"No, not ballet. I was never that coordinated. I was an entomologist, just like your father. Just like Terry. And I'd devoted my life to these ants. Acromyrmex. The leafcutters. They're truly beautiful creatures, easily the pinnacle of social and technological expression in ants. That's what I said in my papers when I was working out of U of M. Cultivated my own nest mounds using a queen and fungi shipped up from the Guanacaste province of Coast Rica.

"I watched that queen every day and saw how hard she worked to grow a culture. Tending to the fungus and her eggs. Aerating soil. Creating a whole new world on her own. It was the most incredible thing I'd ever seen, and I felt something then, something far beyond myself. It faded, but when I saw Yahmuhwesu appear it came back again, and fierce. And whatever that feeling was, he filled me up with it, to the brim. Everything seemed clearer, the interconnectedness of all life, matter, energy, everything. He told me I had a new purpose here, among my 'subjects.' That was the word he used. And when I woke up from whatever fugue I was in, I had become the new queen.

"I could feel them in my brain. Calling to me. Like that buzz you describe. Only it didn't make me itch. It made me...wet. I could feel waves rolling through my belly. I got gooseflesh. My breath ran short. Panting. I buckled twice on the way to the lab and the nest. Because I could hear them. They were still alive. The university's lab was underground and somehow intact. And they needed me. I didn't even think of how I'd abandoned Terry back at the shelter."

"Wait, who is this Terry guy? You were with him when Yahmuhwesu appeared to you?"

"Yeah, but I need to finish telling you about these ants. I think it's important, somehow, that you understand them. Because they are part of me now. They have been ever since I managed to crawl my way through the rubble and get access to the nest mound."

She related the rest of it then, how she'd dug down through the soil and found the existing mother queen and swallowed her whole. How the future mother queens—fledgling tribe-bearers who were meant to eventually carry eggs and fungal spores outward to start new nests—had all crawled to her then, running up her legs, crawling inside of her and resting against the walls of her uterus, triggering orgasms that left her shaking for hours. And after that the rest of the tribe had filed out—tiny food workers/minimas/foragers/soldiers—each finding their place on her body and immediately starting to do their jobs however they could.

"I'm still me. Still Mave," she said, "but now I'm also this colony. My mind contains their hive mind.

"What I don't understand, yet, is what this new fungus is, or why it glows, or why it grows so goddamned fast. Even a hint of it on the jaw of a forager will instantly attach itself to a cutting. That's why the fragments you saw crossing the road were already bright.

"This fungus didn't originate with any of the queens inside; they came to me with nothing other than their instinct.

So...I think the new fungus is coming from *me*. But I don't know how, so I've been holed up here to study it. Some of the ponds and riverbanks near here have vital plant life right at the edge of the water. We need it to really make the colony grow."

"We?"

"Yes, I told you that I'm their queen. I guess I'm using the royal we. And we're the ones who need your help."

He looked at her then, this strange new woman and her legion of tiny ants and her gray/gold eyes. The leafcutters were everywhere on her now, most holding little glowing slivers of plant matter which swayed in the winds and gave her an appearance of profound life, of a majesty that made him want to serve her despite the buzz at the base of his head that was screaming "Run—we can survive best alone."

"What am I supposed to do?"

"That what I'm not quite sure of. I know that we can't stay here much longer, though I'd like to."

"Picket fence?"

"Yeah. That and the nest. But the plant life here was scarce to begin with, and we've already processed most of what remains in the area. Plus, I think Terry might find us."

"Why is that bad?"

"Terry was an entomologist too, before the bombs hit and made everyone's job titles obsolete. That's how I knew him. We both worked out of the university. We were lovers in a purely pragmatic way. We understood the need. The pheromones.

"He was renting an old house in the suburbs south of campus. It was Cold War equipped—bomb shelter in the back yard. We screwed down there for kicks. He wore a gas mask. We passed out holding each other in an army cot and didn't wake up until we felt the concussion of the first bomb exploding. Total dumb luck that we lived.

"Then, when we crawled out a few days later, there was a glowing god waiting for us. Terry could barely handle the shock of all of it. He was crying one second, furious the next. Unstable. Then Yahmuhwesu hummed his way into our heads and changed us. I haven't seen Terry since.

"That's why I'm afraid. Because if Yahmuhwesu affected Terry the same way he did with us, then right now Terry is hunting down a hive of his own."

"More leafcutters?"

"I wish. Terry's bug of choice was the *Nomamyrmex*, Dean. Army ants."

"That's bad?"

"It's terrible. If he manages to find a hive in nature there will be millions of them. And if his mind is as fragile as I believe it to be then Terry will become an instrument of the hive instead of the other way around."

"You don't think he could control them?"

"I don't think he'd even try. He was always so clinical. His brain wasn't equipped for this sort of metaphysical shift. I grew up with hippies in a commune and started meditating with my imaginary friends when I was four years old. I've always desired a more mystical reality, despite my chosen field of work.

"And you, your single-minded drive to stay alive appears to usurp any need for reality.

"But Terry, his brain probably split in two the moment that first bomb dropped and he realized he wasn't ever going to have a cup of Starbucks coffee again."

Dean wanted to laugh, for a moment, but he saw how serious the look in Mave's eyes was. This was dire. The leafcutter ants that covered her were frantic, almost disorganized in their movements.

"Dean, if Terry does unearth a Nomamyrmex colony they'll be *starving*."

"So they'll eat Terry?"

"If we're lucky. But, assuming he's still conscious by then, they'll know what he knows. That there is a veritable smorgasbord waiting for them in the basement of the U of M lab. And when they don't find them there they'll be able to follow our scent trail."

"They eat leafcutters?"

"For centuries the Acromyrmex has been the favorite food of the army ant. Particularly the queens. They'll sacrifice thousands of their fighters in battle to get a good chance at a fat, juicy mother ant. They'll drag her, still living, all the way back to their tunnels, and then slowly pull the eggs from her body and eat them until she collapses and dies. She is consumed last. A victory feast."

Dean saw Mave recoil at this, felt a scared tremor enter the cross-tuned vibrations relaying thought between the two of them.

"Dean, I *am* the Acromyrmex now. I and the colony might be all that is left of us on Earth. And if we can't find a way to move from this place soon, we'll be eaten alive."

8

The long stretch of internal communication had wiped them out but left them wary. Exhausted, they shuffled over to the fence and agreed to sleep in shifts before figuring out how they could travel.

Dean lay near Mave in the lean-to for a few hours, watching the sleepless march of the ants as they moved over her and traveled back and forth to their garden nest. She had been right about the beauty of the creatures. While Dean admired the tenacity and strength of the cockroach, they lacked the grace and civility and immense complexity that made observing the leafcutter such a pleasure.

The roaches knew how to stay alive, but for what? He tried to cut the question off in his mind, knowing the sense of existential dread that was sure to follow any attempted answer.

Dean's father had built up a life for himself. He had done much more than simply "get by." An esteemed figure in his field. Research papers published in all the right magazines. A loving son who helped him through his years as a young widower. But in the end a ridiculous auto accident took his life. His papers and ideas were replaced by newer ones which failed to credit him. His son flipped out and traveled the world squandering the money the father had saved up for years. No, Daddy Dean Sr. had existed for nothing. And now the last of his bloodline was surrounded by semi-empathic roaches and trapped in a wasteland, lying next to a fungus-coated woman with exotic ants in her womb.

Actually, Dean thought, his dad might have been really

intrigued by that last part, but it wasn't what you necessarily hoped for when you had a kid.

After a while Mave opened her eyes (those *eyes*) and within seconds Dean allowed himself to drift into a shallow sleep.

He dreamed—army ants marching/his face consumed by baby roaches/Terry chewing his way through Mave's vagina. He woke screaming. Mave placed her hand on his forehead, the smell of her fungus rich and almost sweet near his nose. He calmed. He caught another hour of shut eye. This time real slumber.

But at waking the dreams still chilled him. They lingered. From the look in *her* eyes, she'd somehow shared his fear.

They hit the road within hours.

Travel time moved on the following agenda:

Head back north, then west when the river branches. Stay close to the water. More likely to find some sort of plant life there. Get far enough west and Mave knew of a place where there might be safety. A military liaison to the university had once been sweet on her and spilled post-coital secrets to impress, including the general location of a military stronghold they'd built out of a natural cave system.

The place was supposed to have some degree of sustainability. Which meant flowing water and clean air. Which could mean weapons with which a person or persons could effectively stave off an invasion of army ants. Which *might* mean a self-contained bio-system that she and Dean could adapt their insectile selves to.

Travel time was a bitch.

They tried to drag part of the Acromyrmex nest behind them on top of her old lean-to tarp. That meant slow-going. That meant frenzied waste workers cleaning out dead ants/collapsed tunnels/reduced gongylidia output. That meant confused foragers hunting dead land for any plant life at all, coming back with empty, ashy mandibles. The fungus across Mave's skin began to lose its luster without new plant life to culture on. The crumbs and trash they tried to adhere to her made her look diseased.

The new queen was upset. Dean would hear her humming, but not in a frequency he could even try to reach. He guessed she was calming the colony; asking them to endure. He knew the sound of her excited his roaches. Their cerci swayed to the sound.

He watched Mave's movements, the sway of her hips, the way her feet seemed to keep moving without real exertion.

For some reason her beauty pitched him double lonely. She would never have a guy like Dean, would she? He considered running ahead, leaving the queen and her dying colony and heading west to the Pacific by himself. She'd only slow him down, maybe even bring a horde of ravenous ants with huge jaws his way.

He could be free. A lone wolf. He'd finally tattoo his knuckles with his motto, four letters across each fist:

DONOTDIE

But was that all he really felt now? He wasn't sure. Those gray/gold eyes kept him unstable.

Maybe we could spend the rest of our time together. Maybe we can find some place with a white picket fence and forty acres out back for nesting.

So for now Dean kept things left foot/right foot/repeat and followed the queen of the dying leafcutters along the river.

9

"It's getting warmer, don't you think? Brighter, too."

Mave had demanded they sit by the river for a while to let her ants search for plant life and harvest proteins from their collapsing nest.

Dean thought she was right about the warmth. He hadn't worn his "Winter Fun" scarf for the last fifteen miles or so. He'd guessed he was heating up from exertion—dragging a backpack full of water and a tarp full of dirt was a gut-buster—but maybe Mave was on point.

He hoped she *wasn't* correct for a few reasons:

One—Dean was sure the cold was all that'd kept the now fantastic number of eggs on his suit from hatching. Currently he and Mave were located nowhere near a worthy stash of baby roach food.

Two—The Nuclear Summer theory. Following nuclear winter the ozone layer and stratosphere are effectively destroyed. UV light would torch any remaining territory that wasn't already turned to desert by the lack of photosynthesis during the blackout. Anything that had a harsh time with UV light before would really feel the burn. Genetic defects galore. Polar ice caps would melt. Continental flooding. The greenhouse effect in fast fast forward. Even sea life would go stagnant, except for those weird things that live off of gas vents at the bottom of the Marianas Trench.

Three—As much as he would welcome a bit of light, it freaked his suit out and ravaged the leafcutter's fungus. They'd both be in even more of a pinch with the sun blazing overhead.

However, he was enjoying the increased sensation of warmth in the air, slight though it was. He laid back against the gentle slope of the riverbank and watched the cancerous clouds churn overhead. He thought, even at this distance from her, that he could smell Mave's fungus. It calmed him. He relaxed his neck, allowing his crash helmet to sink its heft into the ground. His shoulders dropped.

The sound of the river water running seaward formed a constant white noise soundtrack. He let himself float with it, pictured himself as a drop of water, incapable of death, unknowing, yet immensely important and powerful.

He closed his eyes and let his head tip over in Mave's direction.

The smell of her was sort of like lavender mixed with fresh coffee. It invigorated as much as it soothed. Were there spores of it, he wondered, working their way into his brain right now? He hoped so.

She was sovereign. Let him join her subjects, enthralled.

Two sensations:

Movement without control.

The scent of lemons and hot metal. The smell of ruptured ants.

Dean opened his eyes, instantly awake. He was no longer on the riverbank. The roaches were moving at full-out speed, autonomous of his control, heading towards a nearby copse of charred tree stumps.

A scream in the distance—explosive, then suddenly cut off.

Mave.

Dean forced his hands and feet to the ground, churning up hardened earth, leaving tracks. The roaches were not stopping. Whatever they had sensed, they wanted to get as far away as possible.

Go with them, Dean! The roaches got you this far. You can keep living.

You can survive.

Their pace never flagged. Now they were just feet from a low hiding spot.

Another shriek. Crunching sounds that rolled Dean's stomach even at this distance.

You know what's happening, Dean. It's Terry. He's found you. He's found Mave. But he wants to eat her first. A big fat juicy mama ant. Now is your only chance to run!

The suit kept crawling, more cautious now, looking for a way to crest the next hill without being seen by anything down below.

Dean dug his heels in harder but couldn't get traction.

Shit shit shit! Mave's dying. Stop this. Do something.

Dean began to hum. He focused his thoughts on the tight space at the back of his skull and tried to bring the sound as close as he could to the buzz that flourished there.

The roaches began to slow. He let the hum drop to a low drone at the back of his throat. The hive mind buzz locked in.

we are scared we are scared predator scared predator scared distance dark distance quiet scared escape distancehidehidehidehidehideprotecthide

Dean didn't hear actual words, but this was the message he received in a language older than any man had ever created. The language of survival.

It was a sound for animals. It ensured a thriving planet. It was old and powerful and he was sure that a hint of that audible pattern echoed inside of every atom of his body.

But it wasn't anything Dean wanted to listen to anymore.

There was something stronger working through his mind now. A brighter sound at the front of his head. A siren's call.

Her spores really did get into my brain.

Dean tuned into the sound. It felt nearly as ancient as the desire to run, to live at all costs. But this sound had a beauty to it. A nobility.

And as he found the right tone in his throat to harmonize there was only one word at the front of his thoughts:

Fight.

He could smell her and the colony on the poison wind. Sweet fungus. Acidic death. Adrenaline. Pain.

There was another smell in the air, and whether he was pulling it into his mind via his own nose or the roaches receptors he was unsure.

It was the smell of hunger. Desperation.

Dean charged toward it face first, his own feet pushing him onward, workman's boots rubbing his feet raw.

Go in without hesitation. Strike first and then don't stop until she's safe.

He held in a roar, though it raged at the inside of his chest. He let its energy carry him faster.

There—two hundred yards south. A man stood over Mave. Watching her face twist in agony. Her body was covered in moving black shapes, thick ropes of them, orderly lines of assault tearing away at her face/belly/legs.

Nomamyrmex was on the march.

Dean screamed then, hoping the sound would somehow distract even the bugs which were eating away at Mave.

The man—it had to be Terry—rotated to face the sound. He looked right at Dean. One of his eyes was missing. His nose was also absent, replaced by a jagged black triangle bisected by exposed bone.

Despite these obvious deformities, Dean could tell the man was smiling.

Why would he be smili…

The earth fell out from beneath Dean and he felt something long and sharp bore through his right leg before he even realized he wasn't running anymore.

"We're diggers. You cah see that ow. It ohly took us a few hours to displace over six meters of dirt alog this ehtire perimeter. Quite astoudeeg, really."

Terry had approached the pit. The noseless fuck.

"We couldit fide as mady sharp sticks as we'd hoped for, but you do what you cad with what you've got, right? Guess we've lucked out that you hit that particular spike as square as you did. Providess."

Dean said nothing. What good would rage do now? He surveyed his surroundings. Narrow dark rift marked by a million ant trails. A chunk of fractured tree branch jammed through his upper thigh, a few slaughtered roaches hanging from its tip. Wound not bleeding too badly. Must have missed the femoral.

"She told us your name is Dee."

"It's Dean."

"That's what I said. I caht quite make all the sowds I used to. I must admit that we were quite huggry on the trip to fide the Acromyrmex. We had to eat pieces of my face. Other parts too."

At that Terry's remaining eye went wide with fear. Absolute panic.

He emitted a cough, a bark of a low tone. His eye snapped back to empty.

His human brain is still trying to assert itself. Jesus, he's scared. He's so scared, the poor bastard. Those ants are inside of his mind and they've been feeding on him for days.

"Listen, Terry, I know you're in there somewhere. I know you're scared. I know they are hurting you and you're confused and the whole world seems wrong right now, but if you can push to the front of your brain and take control you can stop this. They're just ants."

"Quiet!"

With that Dean noticed the black surge cresting over the lip of the makeshift pit. Thousands—no, hundreds of thousands of them. Thick fingertip-sized ants with bulbous split red-horned heads, each meaty half as big as two whole leafcutters. Their jaw musculature visible from feet away.

Pain is coming, and it will not be brief. If nuclear fallout couldn't kill me how long will it take these ants to end it?

Then he heard the sound. A new tone, from up above. Weak, but coming from Mave.

She's still alive.

He felt, instinctively, that he must try to match her sound.

The first wave of ants was on him. At his earlobes. Sinking their mandibles into the roaches that covered him. Tearing away at his fingertips. Trying to get *into* his fresh wound.

He cleared his throat. He pulled in as much air as he could. Ants bit into his lower lip, sought the meat of his tongue.

From the bottom of his lungs Dean let out his matching tone. It found hers. The sounds merged and became a terrible bellow.

This was a call to war. Dean felt it in his bones.

There was a crackling noise—the sound of thousands of dry distended roach eggs tearing open at once.

Dean's delivery day was here. Within seconds he was the proud father to a seething multitude. The tiny nymphs were too small to be crushed in the huge jaws of the Nomamyrmex, over whom they flowed heedlessly.

They washed up out of the trench, a hungry flood with one target.

Dean stood up, shaking loose hundreds of army ants from his frame. His right leg held. A thick cast of roach nymphs had formed around it, bearing the weight of his broken limb.

He kept his mind focused on Terry. On Terry's face. Those open holes.

Roaches adore dark wet places like that.

Terry turned to run. The nymphs were already halfway up his legs. He made it one stride before the babies had covered his good eye and were piling in to his blasted orbit.

Terry opened his mouth to scream but the only sound Dean could pick up was the rustle of tiny roaches rubbing against each other on their way down the man's throat.

Dean looked away. He hoped they'd kill him soon. He'd tried to focus the nymphs' movement towards Terry's brain but he wasn't sure how long it would take them to chew through to gray matter.

There was a man inside there somewhere. Confused. Violated. Alone.

Shit.

Dean couldn't take it anymore. His suit helped him crawl up out of the pit and over to Terry's twitching body.

Dean shoved one of his gloves in his own mouth. He bit down. He made a two-fisted grab for the sharpened branch that was rammed through his leg. Twisted left. Twisted right. Wailed through a mouthful of wool and leather. Bit down again. Gripped tight. Pulled up and away. Scoped the point of the stick, dripping his own blood, bits of roach still stuck to it.

And then he swung that spear down into Terry's empty eye socket as hard as he possibly could.

10

This is the way Dean looked at it, much later:

One day you go to bed happy. The next day your dad dies. In a stupid, stupid way.

And maybe you give up on the world. Maybe the world forgets you ever existed and you're okay with that. Because you're alive. Not dead. Not anywhere near that sadness again.

Things are easier alone. Nothing to lose = no loss.

But what if *you* die? Isn't that the biggest loss of them all? You're the only one who will ever truly know you were even alive.

So you protect yourself, with a nod to the esteemed Malcolm X, by any means necessary.

But Malcolm, at the moment he'd said that, probably never guessed one of those means would be covering yourself in nasty, nasty insects.

Probably never even came near being a thought in his head.

His loss. Because he's dead now. And you, you just keep living, no matter what the world throws at you. Nuclear weapons, crazy presidents, toxic fallout, man-made gods with nothing better to do than alter the genetic code of the remaining humans on Earth.

Fucking army ants.

Oh, and loneliness. Lots of loneliness. You always have to fight that one. But maybe everybody does.

At least that was a problem when you were human.

But that's not exactly the case anymore, is it?

Back up.

Start again.

One day you fall asleep happy. Next to a river under a dark sky. Then you wake up and everything has changed. Including you. You changed so much that for the first time you actually *risk* your life.

For what?

Love? It's as good a word as any. It'll do.

And you've gone so crazy with this feeling, call it love, that you find yourself in an absurd situation, humming and moaning at telepathic bugs and killing brainwashed entomologists.

I know.

It sounds silly.

But it feels important at the time. So important that you nearly die from blood loss lying there in a desolate field next to a corpse filled with baby roaches.

Again, you fall asleep. Or perhaps you pass out from blood loss. But you're happy. Not totally happy, but feeling like now maybe your life was really a *life*. Something more than rote respiration for as sustained a period as possible.

Then you wake up and everything has changed so goddamned much you think you're in heaven.

But you're not dead, and neither is she. The one you love. Sure, her original right arm is missing (eaten by army ants, you guess), but it appears that some enterprising leafcutter ants have assembled her a new one out of radiant fungus.

These same enterprising bugs have healed up your sundry cuts and wounds and even staved off the infection in your leg with a Streptomyces bacteria that lives on their skin.

A woman once told you these were the best ants on Earth. You now believe her 100%.

As great as those ants are, you might miss your cockroaches.

"I've set them free," she tells you. "They're up there doing what they're meant to do. Making babies and eating death and putting nutrients back into the soil for when the nuclear summer passes and things can grow again."

It's a lot to absorb at once. Losing your friends like that. Finding out the whole Earth has gone Death Valley for the time being. Trying to figure out how this miraculous woman managed to drag your nearly dead coma patient ass all the way out west to these secret caves. But you accept it all after a while.

To fill time, to try to adjust, you write down everything you can remember. Part of you feels like these journals could be the last memories of the extinct species you used to consider yourself a part of.

You might explore your new home. Filters. Generators. Tunnels and tunnels and tunnels. You guess one of them might run right to the center of the Earth, but you never find that particular path.

The woman you love, her favorite place is the sustainable eco-sphere. She can even farm there, next to her ants. But they do a pretty great job without her.

All those rooms—the ones that were supposed to house the soldiers and U.S. officials who weren't ready when the bombs hit—they start filling up with the glowing fungal tufts the ants produce. Aside from that it's dark down there, wherever you want it to be.

One day (or night—who can tell down here?) you fall asleep lonely. Then you wake up the next morning and the woman you love is on top of you. She's lifting her hips and putting you inside of her and making every other Best Moment of Your Life seem pretty pale. And when she's done and you're done you hold each other tight and watch as three luminous Acromyrmex queens emerge from between her legs and crawl up to her belly.

Their wings dry. They shiver/shake/touch antennae.

They take flight.

You can tell that they're headed to the surface—nuclear summer bound.

Their movement through the air is heavy with theft.

This makes the woman you love cry. But she is smiling through the tears. Beaming, really.

For she believes, as you do, that she has just given birth to the first strange children of that terrible new sun.

Jeremy Robert Johnson is the author of *The Loop*, *Skullcrack City*, *Entropy in Bloom*, and *All the Wrong Ideas*. In 2008, he worked with The Mars Volta to tell the story behind their Grammy Award–winning album, *The Bedlam in Goliath*. In 2010 he spoke about weirdness and metaphor as a survival tool at the Fractal 10 conference in Medellin, Colombia. In 2017, his short story "When Susurrus Stirs" was adapted for film and won numerous awards including the Final Frame Grand Prize and Best Short Film at the H.P. Lovecraft Film Festival. He lives in Portland, Oregon.